I0602891

BOOKED FOR HOMICIDE

A SHELF INDULGENCE COZY MYSTERY

S.E. BABIN

OLIVERHEBERBOOKS

Previously published by Sweet Promise Press - 2019

Published by Oliver-Heber Books

0 9 8 7 6 5 4 3 2 1

For coffee who giveth me life and Netflix who giveth me the feels.

WANT TO KEEP UP WITH NEW RELEASES?

You can grab a FREE set of stories here if you sign up for my newsletter.

Or, you can click the kitty cat and follow Sheryl online at sebabin.com. She emails only when she has a new release or has messed something up. And even then she sometimes forgets...

ONE

"Pour me another and keep 'em coming," I said to my assistant, Harper, as she waved the coffee pot at me. I held out my mug like a dutiful soldier, and Harper poured in the life-giving liquid beans that would enable me to get through another day after yet another sleepless night. I rarely had trouble sleeping. I lived a low-stress life surrounded by good books, a gorgeous, uneventful town, and as much coffee as the local handsome supplier could get me to buy. This meant a lot. He was cute, and he used that and his wonderful beans to prey upon my addiction to java. If he didn't move out of this town soon, I was going to have to find a coffee drinker's anonymous group.

I poured in a disturbing amount of cream and a slightly less disturbing amount of sugar and rattled off my daily attack plan to Harper.

"Respond to Jeff's email today with another big fat no."

"Check!" said Harper.

"Re-sort the mystery area. Again." I rolled my eyes. Mrs. Hanson came in again complaining about Jeffery Deaver books getting mixed in with the Agatha Christie's. Considering the old woman kept buying them, I think she was just trying to blame us for her impulsiveness... and her addiction to mysteries a little more hardcore than good ol' Ms. Christie.

"Maybe we should just switch out the jackets so she can buy all the Jeffery Deaver books she wants with zero guilt."

A snort escaped me. "She'll find something else to complain about. Trust me."

Harper poured herself another cup of coffee and leaned against the register. Her blonde hair was done up in a messy bun today, just like it was almost every day. Harper was a low maintenance, low everything kind of girl, but I'd seen her get dressed up on a few occasions and she was a total knock-out. Of course, I always thought she looked great even with her old slogan shirts, skinny jeans and black-framed glasses that made her sparkling green eyes look enormous. But Harper wasn't the kind of person who took compliments graciously. Every time I told her she looked nice, she'd grumble something about not being able to find a hairbrush. I eventually gave up. One day she'd realize the male traffic we had pouring in and out of here on the weekends had a lot less to do with books and a lot more to do with her.

Until then, she was doing a lot for our bottom line because whatever book Harper recommended to those hapless males, they'd happily buy. I learned to keep my amusement to myself over it. Harper was a smart girl, a wonderful employee, and a massive bookworm.

You kind of had to be to work in a shop like this one. Tattered Pages focused on the new, quirky, and the rare. We could order whatever books you needed if we didn't already have it in stock, and you could read here if you wanted. I made a point of setting up several comfy lounge areas scattered around the store. There were bean bag chairs, recliners, hardback chairs for the strict, and even a small meditation area scattered with zafu cushions and soft pillows.

One thing I didn't have and was working toward was a small eating area where people could order some coffee and something sweet with their purchase. I hoped to have that up and running within the next few months. Then my dream of owning a bookshop/small cafe would finally be realized.

The other resident of the bookshop sprung up onto the counter and promptly rubbed herself against Harper's arm. She reached over and gave Poppy a scratch behind the ears. The red Persian came with the store after the old owner passed away. She'd been made part of the sale which I hadn't been too happy about, but Poppy turned out to be a welcome addition to the Tattered Pages family. The townspeople loved her and, as cats were wont to do, she tolerated them back.

A lot of things had changed for me since I plunked down my entire savings to buy the store. I'd knocked down a few walls and completely renovated the place. I sold most of the stock and replenished it with my own choices. Rare books were kept under lock and key, fitted with a screeching alarm just in case someone tried to pry it open. Nothing like that really happened around Silverwood Hollow, but I wasn't originally from here, so better safe than sorry for me. I'd grown up several towns away but had lived here for close to ten years now.

My shop was nestled between a cupcake shop and a specialty oil shop. I frequented both of them because: a) I loved cupcakes and b) specialty oils were cool, and the owner made fresh bread every single day and offered it up as samples to dip in the oil.

I could not resist the bread and it was obvious from the extra fifteen pounds I carried around. I didn't mind much. If I gave up bread, I gave up joy. No one wants to give up joy. So, I continued popping over there a few times a week to see what new thing Jenny had to offer and what new bread recipe she managed to come up with.

Plus, I loved the name, *Olive Twist!*

The cupcake shop was another demon of its own. I frequented that one almost every day, much to my own chagrin. In my defense, she moved in after I'd bought the store and renamed it. Otherwise, I probably would have found a new location away from such tasty temptation. Sprinkle Heaven was just that. Delicious, frosted heaven.

Trudy was a wizard when it came to cupcakes. From the traditional to the downright bizarre, she cornered the market on unique when it came to the tiny cakes. Plus, even though I couldn't keep my hands off her treats, she sent business into the store all the time just because people liked to shop after they ate something delicious.

Poppy abruptly dropped and rolled over, exposing her belly to Harper. She grinned and quickly scratched her belly. With Poppy you never knew exactly how much petting she could take before she swiped you with a paw. She was a temperamental beast, but she kept the kids entertained when they came in. It was all I could ask for, really.

Harper sipped her coffee. "Anything else you want me to do today?"

I shrugged. "I don't think so. Everything should be good until Friday. Then we have to get ready for the twenty percent off sale. Plus, we have the festival coming up. Maybe we should start brainstorming some ideas for that."

The Silverwood Hollow Harvest Festival was hands down the primo event of the season. People came from all over to attend. It was chaotic but wonderful and I loved every second of it. Volunteers signed up to help decorate the town square and almost all the shop owners worked together to decorate their shops in the same theme. There were always a couple of hold outs. Craig, the old curmudgeon who owned the custom knife shop, never decorated, and we finally had to stop asking him after he threatened to start throwing knives at us.

This town was full of colorful characters. Lucky for me, I liked weird people.

Harper's eyes lit up. She adored fall and all of its wonderful things. "We should have a bake-off. The grand prize winner gets a big basket of books and a $50 gift certificate for the shop."

My gaze narrowed as I thought about it. "It could work. Should we make it a little more specific than that? Maybe make it pies? Or fall desserts?"

Harper straightened. "Ooh and have an additional category for best use of cinnamon or cloves!"

"Maybe we could add in a fall-drink category." I tapped my chin as I thought about it. "We'd have to keep an eye on Corky if we allowed alcohol in."

A smirk lit up Harper's face. Corky was my aunt on my mother's side. I loved her to death, but she was a handful, especially when she whipped her flask out. My mom and I hid the thing at least once a week, but it didn't matter if Corky found it or not. The next time we'd see her, she'd have a brand-new flask and the same sparkle of mischief in her eyes.

"Does it really matter if we had alcohol or not considering she's going to bring it in anyway?" Harper snickered. She, like most of the population of this town, adored Corky, but her shenanigans had the potential to be really embarrassing. Plus, I didn't think she even sipped out of the flask. I suspected she kept it as a prop and as an excuse to act outrageous.

"We'll just have to watch her," I said and sighed. "Let's get it all down on paper and present it to the other stores around here. Maybe we can get them in on it, or at least see if they want to donate anything."

"Like cupcakes?" Harper asked, her eyes wide and innocent. She knew exactly how much I loved those Sprinkles cupcakes.

"Maybe," I said and winked at her.

The bell over the door jingled merrily, and we both turned to see who'd come in. Tattered Pages had a loyal following in the town, but we also got a lot of traffic from tourists. Some seasons were busier than others.

Fall was arriving in Virginia, and with it came the changing of the leaves from bright green to dark reds and burnt oranges. The weather was pretty constant and stayed at a brisk fifty something degrees during the month of October. November, when the harvest festival was scheduled, would dip down into a cool forty something. Harper and I were both wearing a long sleeve shirt and a zipped up over vest. Every time the door opened, a brisk wind would blow into the store, shifting our hair and freezing our noses.

It wasn't too cold yet. That honor would save itself until around Christmas time and we Virginians were a hardy stock.

Jen from *Olive Twist!* stepped in and with her came the smell of warm, yeasty bread and something with garlic. Like Pavlov's dog, my mouth started to water.

"Garlic?" I said, perking up and sniffing the air. "What is that?"

Jen, pretty and perky for so early in the morning,

grinned as the door shut behind her. "It's my new garlic rye loaf." In her late forties, Jen was slim and fit. Her light hair was just starting to silver at the edges of her hairline, but her complexion was still wrinkle-free and smooth. Her face was round, and her cheeks were tinged pink by the cool air.

She smacked my hands away gently as I started to reach for it. "Hold your horses," she said as she walked over to the counter. Steam rose from the brown paper bag as she opened it and slid the bread out. Placing it on top of the bag, she dug around in her purse and pulled out a small knife.

"Always prepared!" she announced. Jen sliced through the bread, cutting two generous slices and handed one to me and Harper, who'd followed behind me.

I snagged mine greedily and took a huge bite. Buttery, garlic goodness burst on my tongue and I stifled a moan. Bread was one of my major vices, but it was one hard to feel guilty about. The other was my habit of weekend, pajama wearing Netflix binges. Both were bad for my waistline.

Jen stared at us in anticipation. "What do you think? I want to introduce this next week and maybe put it in rotation as a menu item."

I perked up at that. "You're going to start selling bread?"

"Sure am," she agreed.

"That's going to be terrible for my waistline and wallet," I said. "But delicious for my belly," I added to soften my words.

"It's a natural progression," Jen said as she lay the knife

down on top of the paper bag. "I've been selling oils for so long and making the bread just as a hobby, but for years people have been asking me where to get the bread from." Her shoulder lifted and fell in a slight shrug. "Thought I might as well give them what they're asking for."

"I can't wait," Harper said around a mouth full of bread. "This is wonderful."

"The garlic came from the Coon's farm up the road," Jen said. "Seasonal, so I have to stock up and make sure I store it properly." A frown touched her brow. "If I do it wrong, I'm stuck using grocery store garlic, and it just isn't the same."

I cut myself another slice of the dark rye bread. "Whatever you're doing, keep it up. This is amazing."

"You girls keep the rest of that," she said and waved as she adjusted the purse over her shoulder. "I have to get back to the shop."

My mouth dropped open. "You're leaving us the whole loaf? That's a terrible thing to do, Jen!"

Her laugh echoed in the store as she swept out of the shop, the bell jingling as the door opened.

I stared down in dismay at the garlic rye loaf.

Harper snorted in amusement. "There's this thing..." Harper began. "It's called willpower."

I waved the knife at her. "Don't judge me. This is delicious bread."

I cut myself another slice and swore I'd eat salad for dinner.

Life was all about balance.

TWO

Two hours before the shop closed, I was on my hands and knees sorting through a box of used books someone had just brought into the store. For the most part, people around here didn't drop off things too damaged to be used. Sometimes, though, we had people using our store as a dumping ground.

This box seemed to be a combination of it. The girl who dropped it off was young, probably early twenties and claimed to be from out of town. She was fixing a place up to make it a rental property and pulled the books out of one of the extra bedrooms. She barely waited around for me to give her a receipt and seemed to have zero interest in the contents.

I pulled out three water damaged books - two of which were too soaked through to be legible. The third might be salvageable so I set it aside.

I ran my hands through the box, quickly moving books

to the side and out of the way. It was only when I got to the bottom that my hands started to shake.

"No way," I whispered as I pulled out a copy of The Great Gatsby. The hardcover was bright blue with a pop of red on the spine.

If this was what I thought it was ...

I cracked open the book carefully, my gloved fingers holding the book with the reverence it deserved, and gasped.

It was signed and the printing date was 1925. I scanned the copyright page, holding my breath until my gaze lit on what I was looking for.

I held it up like Rafiki held up Simba when he was announcing the new king and let out a little screech.

"Dakota?" Harper asked, her voice concerned. Her head poked around the corner. Harper's eyes widened and her mouth formed a little O of surprise.

"No way," she echoed. "Is that?"

I nodded, my head wobbling around in excitement. "It is. A first edition." I lowered my voice. "And signed."

Harper came around the corner full speed and collapsed down beside me on her knees. "May I?" she asked.

"Not until you get some gloves on," I admonished.

Harper's cheeks colored pink. "Of course." She rushed around and rummaged underneath the counter. When she came back, I handed over the book. Harper carefully opened it. Tears shimmered in her eyes.

"This is amazing."

"And worth a bundle," I added unnecessarily. I had to look it up to be sure, but I thought this would run for over ten grand.

"Should we call them back?" Harper asked anxiously.

My eyes widened. "Are you insane?" I hissed. "No way. This is like finding a Rembrandt at a garage sale. Freely given and all that." I got off my knees with a groan and stood up. "Plus, I've already given them the tax sheet. It's ours."

Harper looked doubtful, but I shook my head. That was business. Never give away anything you haven't investigated. Nine times out of ten it was kids going through their parents' effects and giving things away because they no longer had the room. Those times were when we got the best treasures. This generation was different. A lot of times they didn't realize what they actually had and didn't take the time to figure it out. They just wanted to go back to normal.

It was sad, really, but we benefited from it more often than not. Harper handed the book back to me, and I carried it to the back. We kept a safe in the office for things like this, though this was the first time something this valuable had landed in our laps from a donation box. I didn't want it to get misplaced, which was easy to do in a store full of books. The doorbell jingled while I crouched to open the safe.

Harper could handle whatever came in, so I continued opening the combination lock. The safe had just clicked open when Harper opened the office door. Her face was a mix of annoyance and anger.

I frowned as I looked up at her. "Everything okay?"

"Jeff is here," she said, her words short and clipped.

I sighed and carefully slid the book into a breathable cloth sack. I tucked it into the safe, on top of some important papers and shut the door to the safe. I double checked to make sure it locked properly and stood up, wiping dust off my knees.

"Did he say what he wanted?" I asked as I held the door open for her to walk back out.

"Nope. He insisted he see you, though." Harper brushed past me in a cloud of floral scented perfume, anger etched into every step she took.

I never believed in the concept of an arch nemesis until I met Jeff Bastian. I hadn't been the owner of my shop for a week before he barreled in asking me to name my price. He'd arrived in town right after I locked myself into the deal to buy the store and had been hounding me ever since to sell the place. I wasn't sure how many different ways I could tell the man no before he left me alone, but so far nothing had worked.

I stepped into the main area of the store and Jeff spun around. His brown eyes did that thing that some guys with no respect for women did. The look at your face then skim quickly down your entire body with their gaze in less than a second. As if he could tell I'd just been stuffing my face with Jen's delicious homemade bread. I stifled a shudder and put on my best bored look.

"Hi, Jeff. The answer is still no."

Jeff's lips thinned. "As delightful as I find you, Dakota, that isn't why I'm here."

Surprise sent my brows up to my hairline. "Oh? That's a first. Are you looking for something in particular?"

Jeff sniffed and turned his nose up. He was such a snob. "My brother is visiting soon. He's thinking about moving here. I'd like to get him a guidebook of Virginia."

Jeff here for a book? Wonders would never cease. "Two Bastians in the town of Silverwood Hollow?" I said. "I'm not sure my poor heart can handle it."

"Funny," Jeff said, his voice unamused. His gaze flicked around the store, taking in all the ambiance. He didn't seem like a guy who enjoyed ambiance. Jeff seemed like the type to stomp all over ambiance, like a greedy Godzilla rampaging through the town. He was the kind of guy who wanted to tear my shop down and replace it with some-thing that looked exactly like the shop next to it. "So, have you visited Jen yet?" I gave him an innocent smile. I wasn't the only one Jeff was bugging to sell. He wanted all the shops on this side of the town. For what, none of us knew, but it couldn't be good.

He rolled his eyes. "Guidebook, Dakota, before I go to the big box store out of town."

I put a hand to my heart. "The horror," I said dryly and waved at him to follow me.

Jeff pushed off the counter and walked beside me, his dry lemonish cologne tickling my nose. "Tell me about your brother," I asked as we walked.

His gaze lit on me, but he looked away. "Totally different from me. Fancies himself somewhat of an artist. I think you'll like him."

I thought I might, too, but the way Jeff said it didn't make it seem like a compliment. "What type of artist?" I led him through the back of the store to the reference section. I kept several guides of Virginia in stock because of the tourists.

"Seascapes," Jeff said. "I think. He does some sculpture work, too."

I stopped at the shelf I needed and ran my fingers over the spines. "Is that what he does full-time?"

Jeff sighed. "No, he's a librarian."

My fingers stilled, and I pulled back to look up at Jeff. His height was imposing. I knew this was irritating him, so I wanted to draw it out. "Really? A librarian?"

A smile was about to curl his lips, but he stifled it. I couldn't believe stuffed shirt Jeff had a librarian brother.

"Yes," he said shortly. "Like I said. You'll like him. But he's a huge disappointment to our family."

I rolled my eyes at that. Even Jeff sounded like he didn't believe that one. Turning back to the guides, I pulled one of them out entitled, *Virginia's Best and Yummy.*

"This one has all the tourist spots, plus a guide of the best places to eat. Has he ever been here?"

Jeff shook his head. "No, we're all from California. This will be the first time he's been here."

"Then this should work. If he wants any books while he's here, please tell him to stop by."

Jeff plucked the book out of my fingers. "He's a librarian," he sneered. "He has plenty of books."

The man in front of me obviously didn't understand how books worked. "Okay then. Since you were halfway human today, have Harper ring you up at regular price."

His brow furrowed. "Regular price?"

"Yup," I said, as I waggled my fingers at him. "We have a list of Jeff prices dependent on how annoying you are to us."

Jeff snorted and headed up to the register. I grinned at his back. I certainly didn't like the guy, but maybe there was more than meets the eye to him.

I watched as Harper rang him up. She eyeballed him a few times, I assume waiting for him to make a sarcastic comment, but he didn't. When he took his bag, she turned to me and I shrugged having no explanation for his out of character behavior. Maybe his meds kicked in. No idea.

Two women brushed past Jeff and into the store before the door closed behind him. They were both short, dark-haired, and bore a remarkable resemblance to one another. Familiarity tickled at the back of my mind. I knew I'd seen them somewhere before. Silverwood Hollow was a small town, but not everyone here read a lot. Plus, I had a lot of competition from the neighboring towns with larger bookstores. I wasn't too worried about it, though. I was doing a comfortable, brisk business here. Plus, I could get my hands on books the bigger stores couldn't.

"Hi!" I greeted. "Welcome to Tattered Pages."

The shorter woman smiled at me, a bright grin lighting

up her round, pleasant face. Her skin was weathered from the sun, but there were dark circles under her eyes, suggesting more of an issue than just a few sleepless nights. "Hello," she said. "I keep saying I'm going to come in here, but I rarely feel well enough to leave the house these days." She pointed outside. "But it's just so breezy and cool today that I felt I had to get out!"

I smiled back, not wanting to pry into her health issues. But curiosity made me say, "I'm sorry to hear that, but I'm glad you're here. Is everything okay with your health?"

I glanced over to the woman standing next to her. A dark frown wrinkled her brow before it quickly disappeared.

The friendly woman waved a hand. "Oh, it comes and goes, you know? Some days I feel okay. Some days I'm just tired. All part of getting old, I guess." She put a hand on her companion's shoulder. "This is my sister, Carrie, and I'm Marcy."

I knew they had to be related. I smiled politely and stuck out my hand. "Dakota Adair. I own this shop."

Marcy shook my hand. Her hands were freezing. Sadness squeezed my heart as I felt the tremor of her grip. When she released it, I waited for Carrie to shake, but she didn't make a move to, so I dropped my hand awkwardly.

The other woman was taller and thinner, her face sharp in its edges. I wondered if she ever smiled. She put a proprietary hand on her sister's elbow and muttered a low "excuse me."

I stepped out of the way and let her pass, a frown

forming on my face as I watched them. Something was weird about those two, the taller sister more than the friendlier one. Shaking my head, I wandered back behind the counter. Harper was still standing there, her gaze trailing after the two women.

"They were kind of weird, weren't they?" Harper whispered.

I nodded. "Definitely. It takes all kinds, though, and if they're here to buy, then we should sell to them." I shrugged but still watched them as they rounded a corner.

Poppy jumped on top of the counter and rubbed against my arm. I stroked her silky head. Her attention was rapt in the area where the woman disappeared to and just before she jumped down, a hiss erupted from her small body.

My eyebrows rose as I watched the cat stick her tail straight up in the air and sashay over to the area where they were.

"She won't bite anyone, will she?" Harper asked, concern thick in her voice.

I blinked. "I wouldn't think so. She's never bitten anyone unless they pet her for too long. Even then it's usually just a snap to get them to stop." My gaze trailed after Poppy as she disappeared around the corner. "Let's hope."

About ten minutes later, the women came up to the counter. "I'm looking for Alice in Wonderland," Marcy said.

Harper stepped around the desk. "We have it in the

back with the children's books," she said. "Would you like me to escort you?" She pointed to the right corner of the store where all the young adult fiction was shelved.

Carrie, the taller sister, shook her head. "No. She's looking for a rare version. It's Through the Looking Glass." She sent a dirty look over to Marcy. "Not the first one. She's looking to complete the set."

Harper blinked and dropped her hand. "Okay then," she said and pressed her lips together.

Marcy's cheeks flushed pink at her sister's behavior. "So sorry," Marcy said as she sent her sister a disapproving look. "I was willed our parent's books about five years ago, and we've been looking for the other book for quite a while. I didn't realize your store might stock it until I was at the library and I overheard someone talking."

Carrie's gaze narrowed, but she didn't speak again. I squashed down a trickle of intense dislike for her and turned my attention to Marcy. "I know we don't have that book in stock, but I can try to get it in for you. What's your budget?"

Marcy sighed. "I'm not really sure. I'm more of a reader than a collector. I have a lot of rare books at my home, but the only reason I have them is because they were given to me." A sad smile lit her mouth. "I'd much rather be reading them than storing them." She sighed. "Isn't that what books are for?"

Carrie gave a derisive snort.

I reached over and patted Marcy's hand. "Of course it is. We use special gloves to handle any rare books coming in, but even we get tempted to snuggle down in one of those bean bags and get lost in the world of fiction."

Gratefulness flickered in her eyes. "I guess we can look and see. Ideally I'd like to keep the costs low if I can."

"You can't possibly hope to spend less than a grand on the book you need," Carrie snapped. "It won't look right sitting next to the first edition!"

My eyebrows went up a little at that. They had a first edition of Alice in Wonderland?

Marcy sighed a patient sigh. "I don't care about that, Carrie. I just want the set completed, just to have the two books. It doesn't matter what edition it is."

"But it does," she whined. "It will look terrible."

Marcy shook her head. "The house is already stuffed to the gills with books. No one will even notice."

Carrie pressed her lips together so tightly they went white.

Marcy continued. "I had to move most of the books to the inside of my master bedroom." She shook her head. "It's stuffed floor to ceiling with books! I have new flooring being installed in a day or two and they needed everything out."

"Oh, that's wonderful!" I said politely. "What kind of flooring?"

"Just some laminate," Marcy said. "It looks pretty, though, and I got a wonderful deal on it through a friend!"

I bent over the keyboard and began to type in the search parameters to find her book. There were a lot listed. "The cheapest one I can find is about $250. The condition is good, but I wouldn't handle it without gloves. Is that a good price point?" I turned the screen so she could see it.

"No," Carrie said quickly. "It just won't do."

Marcy stood up straighter and faced her sister. "I don't think that's up to you, now is it?" she said.

Carrie's eyes widened in surprise and something dark glittered in her eyes. A shiver ran up my spine. Her sister was truly unlikeable.

"I suppose not," Carrie mumbled.

Marcy leaned over to peer at the book for sale. "That looks like it will do," she said. "Would you mind looking around a little more for me? I'm afraid I'm not feeling very well, so I need to go. But if you find something in a comparable price point in better condition would you mind snagging it for me?"

"Of course," I said. Hurriedly thumbing through the files I kept on the side of the register, I pulled a form out and quickly wrote down the book Marcy was looking for and her estimated budget.

"This is a short contract between you and me just stating if I order the book, you will reimburse the purchase price." We didn't often do that, but we had the capability to. Marcy seemed like a woman who would keep her word. Plus, she wanted the book just because she loved it and not for how valuable it was.

I handed her over the pen, and she signed her name in a quick flourish. Straightening, she gave me a weak smile and turned to go.

I raised my hand in farewell. "I'll be in touch," I said.

At that moment, Poppy jumped up on the counter and sat there staring at the two women, her look fixated on the taller sister.

"Oh!" Carrie said. "Adorable kitty." She reached out to give Poppy a stroke on the head, but the cat hissed and swiped at her with her paw. I inhaled a gasp and Carrie took a step back.

Without a word, Carrie took her sister by the arm and escorted her out the door. She turned once before she walked out of the shop and gave me an unreadable look.

I hoped when the book came in that Marcy came in to pick it up herself. I didn't think I wanted to see that woman again. From Poppy's reaction, she didn't want to either.

THREE

It took a week for the woman's book came in. I did the best I could to try to find something in really good condition and at the price point she wanted. As soon as I slid out of my car, I shivered in the cold fall air and zipped my jacket up a little higher to cover my mouth and nose.

The woman's house was waterfront property, nondescript but well-kept. It was painted a soft blue and had an inviting wrap-around porch attached to it. A lonely rocking chair sat next to the door, its paint peeling off. A planter was off to the right of the chair, but the plant inside of it had long since died. Although the house was cheery from a distance, walking closer to it showed there were real signs of neglect. Sadness hit me as I walked up to the steps. The porch itself was made of wood and was probably once gorgeous, but the paint had long since peeled and the wood bleached to a pale imitation of what it had once been.

Inhaling a sigh, I reached up and knocked on the door,

hopeful that what I had in the sack slung over my arm would make her happy. It was right at the top of her budget, unsigned, but in almost pristine condition. The color and spine of the book would closely match the one she had, even if it wasn't worth as much. Still, Marcy admitted she wasn't much of a collector and just wanted the book for the joy it would bring her. Carrie would hate it.

A smile lit my lips over that thought. Carrie probably hated a lot.

The seconds stretched longer until I knocked again. It might take her a while to come to the door, especially if she wasn't feeling well.

I shifted back and forth on my feet in an effort to keep warm. Foggy breath puffed from me. I leaned against the doorframe and listened for footsteps.

Nothing.

I frowned and knocked one more time, this time slipping off my glove to make sure my knuckles made contact with the door. Stepping back, I looked around the small neighborhood. There weren't too many houses on the street. Most of them, including Marcy's, had a large plot of land with it. Behind it, the waters of Silverwood Bay gently washed against the shore. Briny and clean air swirled around me, gently lifting my hair.

I loved it here. The people, the gorgeous bay, the sweet taste of fresh seafood right off the coast. There was little I would change about it, even if I could.

I blew out a huff of frustrated air. There was still no

answer and Marcy had sworn she'd be home today. I called her this morning to double check. I walked to the side of the porch and peeked around toward the back. An old, gray Honda sat quietly in the driveway.

"Hmmm," I muttered. I hoped nothing was wrong. I went back to the door, knocked one more time. If I didn't hear someone calling, I'd take more drastic measures. Normally, I'd leave and try again later, but Marcy was excited about the new book and we'd agreed to meet at three this afternoon. I dug my cell phone out of my bag and punched the last number I called into it.

The phone jangled inside. Once. Twice. Again until the voicemail picked up.

"Shoot," I whispered. I headed over to the large windows and peeked in through the slight gap the curtains made. The house was dimly lit, but I couldn't see anything amiss through the first one.

Maybe she'd forgotten.

I walked to the second window on the other side of the door and peeked through that one, too. Squinting through the curtains gap, my heart sped up as my brain tried to register what I was seeing.

I pounded on the window. "Marcy!" I shouted.

Someone, maybe Marcy, was lying on the floor. I could make out two feet encased in house slippers, but the rest of the person was obscured by a wall.

I rushed away from the window and tried the door handle. To my surprise, the door opened right away. I stepped back like something bit me and froze as I pondered going in.

She could be hurt. I should try to help her.

She could be dead, and I might mess up an investigation. A few seconds later, I pushed open the door and went inside. My urge to help her if she was hurt overrode the police concerns. In an emergency, even a few moments could make or break someone's life. As soon as I stepped in, I reeled back at a strange smell. Cloying, sweet and something I remember vaguely smelling before. I covered my mouth with the crook of my arm and pushed through. The living room floor was halfway replaced with a dark laminate. The rest of it was sitting in a neat pile by the door. Maybe the crew had taken the day off.

Bad timing for Marcy if they had. I jogged over to the person and crouched down.

My breath caught. It was Marcy.

Shivering, I put two fingers to the side of her neck to feel for a pulse, but I knew what I would find.

Nothing.

Marcy was dead.

MY TEETH CHATTERED as I hurriedly stepped back and fumbled through my bag again for my cell. Dialing 9-1-1, I stepped out of the house and sank into the old rocking chair. Poor Marcy.

"9-1-1, please state your emergency," a monotone voice said over the line.

I rattled off what had happened and the address I was at.

"Please stay where you are, and we will send help shortly. Are you sure the woman is deceased?"

"Positive," I said glumly. "No pulse and ..." I swallowed hard. "Her coloring is off. She's definitely dead."

"Okay," the operator said. "Hang tight. Help will be there soon." The operator left the line open, and I punched the speaker button on my cell so I could put the phone down.

I dug out a small vial of hand sanitizer I kept in the bottom of my purse and squirted a large amount on my hands. I'd never touched a dead body before, but I knew I never wanted to again. The book in my satchel sat like a dead weight against my shoulder, so I shrugged the bag off and set it on the ground next to me. I couldn't return it.

I sighed at the thought but immediately felt guilty at the reason why I couldn't return it. The poor woman. I wondered what kind of health problems she had. I hadn't seen any blood, so it looked like whatever it was might have taken her out. Heart attack, maybe?

I scrubbed a hand over my face. I had no idea. All I wanted to do was get out of here and let the police do their job.

Less than a minute later, an ambulance with the lights on pulled up, followed by two patrol cars. I stood up, sliding my purse over my shoulder, and waited for the police to come up the porch. Two EMT's jumped out of the ambulance and pulled a stretcher from the back. I didn't recognize them, but that wasn't surprising. I'd only visited the Silverwood Hollow hospital a couple times, and I'd been much younger then.

The EMT's wheeled the stretcher up to the home and gave me a quick nod as they walked past me. One of them was tall with chestnut hair. He looked maybe late twenties; his handsome face flushed with the cold. The other was shorter, a little rounder, and had a head full of curly dark hair. His blue eyes flashed as they took me in and he offered me a nod as well, though he didn't seem as friendly.

I watched them walk into the house and saw the curly-haired guy's nose crinkle as the weird odor got to him, too. My lips quirked once before I sobered my expression. This didn't seem like the time to be amused by anything.

The sound of car doors closing brought my attention to the officers. The first, a taller, older gentleman walked up the stairs with a practiced swagger and stood in front of me.

"Miss Adair?" he questioned, his light brown eyes flicking over my face.

I nodded. "I was the one who called in." Obviously. Duh. He already knew that.

The other officer right behind him, pressed his lips together but not before I saw the upward tilt of them. He thought I was funny? Great.

"I'm aware," the first officer said. He was a few inches taller than me, but that wasn't saying much because I barely topped five foot three. His hair was hidden mostly by the hat he wore, but it looked to be dark. The man's skin was olive, and his face was classically handsome. "Can you tell me what happened?"

My gaze went to the other officer who hadn't introduced himself. "Who's this?" I asked before I started my story again.

The officer frowned. "This is newly minted Detective Cavanaugh," he said, his lips curled in distaste. Either Detective Cavanaugh was not well-liked, or this officer had something personal against him.

"Why is he wearing a police uniform?" I asked. I knew enough about the police force to know detectives usually showed up in regular clothes.

"It's his last day," the officer said shortly. "He starts tomorrow."

Detective Cavanaugh pushed forward and extended his hand. "Pleasure, Miss Adair. I'll be working here and in the surrounding counties when the need comes up, but today I'm all yours."

My cheeks reddened at his possibly unintentional innuendo. The detective's devilish blue eyes sparkled as he saw me register his words. I put my gloved hand in his and shook. "It's nice to meet you."

Cavanaugh made a motion toward the officer. "That's Officer Clarke. He's always cranky so don't mind him."

"Watch yourself, Cavanaugh," Clarke warned. His eyes snapped with annoyance.

"I'm here to observe, but until tomorrow Clarke here is in the lead. I'll stay here to listen to your statement and then head inside. Whenever you're ready." Cavanaugh reached into his front pocket and pulled out a small notepad and a pencil.

I stared between the two men and frowned before I began to speak. There really wasn't much to tell. When I finished, Cavanaugh shoved the notepad back into his pocket. Clarke was the one who asked the questions.

"Did you see anyone else around here before you came?" He clicked his pen a couple of times.

I shook my head. "Just me."

"Did you hear anything inside?" Clarke's voice was firm and no-nonsense.

"Only when I called her phone." My lips twitched.

He stiffened when he realized I was being sarcastic. "Anything else?" he practically barked.

"Nothing." I told him about our standing appointment and how I hadn't realized anything was wrong until I looked in the windows.

"So, you just went inside?" he said, his tone disapproving.

A huff of breath escaped Cavanaugh. When our eyes met, he rolled his behind Clarke's back. Keeping my expression blank, I nodded. "I thought she might be in need of assistance. Since I could only see her feet, I couldn't tell what might be wrong."

Another car pulled up to the curb and a woman wearing a dark purple suit got out. Her heels clacked on the sidewalk as she came up to the porch in a hurry.

A frown creased his brow. "And what do you think might be wrong?"

I tilted my head to study him. "Well, I thought she might be dead, Officer Clarke."

A bark of laughter escaped Cavanaugh. Clarke turned to glare at him. "These are necessary questions, Miss Adair."

The woman in purple spoke. "I think they aren't, Officer Clarke. The manner of death is for me to decide." Her eyes flashed with annoyance. She was taller than me but shorter than Clarke even in heels. Her dark hair was styled perfectly in waves down past her shoulders and her makeup perfectly applied in the natural style, so it looked dewy and not overdone.

She stuck a hand out, and I shook it, feeling the warmth of her palm even through my gloves. "I'm Madeleine Corsair, the Medical Examiner for Silverwood Hollow." She rolled her eyes at Clarke. "I was on my way to a conference out of town but got this call and had to divert." An apologetic smile graced her mouth. "It's a small town and if I left now, we wouldn't have answers for days. Hopefully this is nothing more than natural causes."

Officer Clarke hissed in his breath. "Madeleine..." he warned.

"Oh hush. Nothing bad ever happens in this town." Madeleine gave me a small wave and opened her bag. She pulled out something plastic and opened them up. "Booties," she said as she bent down to slide them over her shoes.

"The EMT's already went in," I said unhelpfully.

"They needed to make sure there were no signs of life,"

she said. "The two that went in are smart, though." She looked at Clarke. "Good job on getting those two. If something happened in there other than natural causes, they'll be careful to preserve the evidence."

I blinked. "Good to know," I said. "I guess."

Madeleine winked and went inside the home.

"Can I go now?" I asked, impatient to get back to my store and let these people get on with their work.

"I have just a few more questions," Clarke said.

I sighed and nodded. "Okay." I turned back around and settled myself in the rocking chair. I wanted to help with Marcy but being here was making me edgy. Pulling my wallet out, I got two business cards out and handed them to Cavanaugh and Clarke. "I own Tattered Pages. If you ever need to get a hold of me, you can find me there."

The men took the cards, and I waited for Clarke to finish interrogating me. He wouldn't have called it that probably, but it's what it felt like.

Cavanaugh nodded at me and followed Madeleine inside the home.

I'D JUST GATHERED my things and was heading down the steps when a man stepped out from behind a car. I yelped and skittered away from him, holding my purse up like I was going to knock him over the head with it.

"Whoa," he said and held his hands up in surrender. "Sorry. Sorry! I didn't want them to see me."

"Who?" I questioned.

"The cops," the man said sheepishly.

I let go of my bag and stared at the man suspiciously. "Excuse me? Who are you?" He stood several inches taller than me. His frame was lean like he was a runner or a swimmer. Dressed casually in jeans and a gray long-sleeved polo, he looked out of place at the house now that it was overrun with the authorities. His hair was a sandy blond and ruffled by the cold breeze. Light green eyes were highlighted by a pair of black wire-framed glasses. He was cute in a geeky sort of way.

Men like him were my Kryptonite. If he had a big vocabulary, I might be toast. I'd never seen him before, but that didn't mean much considering this was my first potential crime scene. Certainly, the first time I'd ever been on scene during an investigation.

"Cole Gardener," he said. He didn't offer to shake my hand. His were stuck in his pockets. I just realized the guy wasn't wearing a jacket.

"Aren't you cold?" I frowned at his appearance.

"Freezing," he admitted sheepishly, "but I was in a hurry to get over here especially when I heard there was a witness."

I took a step back. "Excuse me? How could you know that?"

"Police scanner," he admitted.

"Who are you? And I don't just mean your name." I pulled my purse closer to me. "If you don't tell me who you are, right now, I'm going to scream."

Alarm registered in his face. "No!" He waved his hands

in a frantic gesture and lowered his voice to a whisper. "I'm a journalist for the Silverwood Hollow Gazette."

A frown twisted my mouth. He was just nosy, then. An annoyed sigh escaped me. He might be cute, but I wanted nothing to do with a news story. Silverwood Hollow was a small town and something like this was sensational. If he printed anything with my name on it, I'd never hear the end of it around here. I liked my life clean and drama-free, thank you very much. My mother would never let me live it down if she had to find out what I'd been involved in through the local newspaper.

"No comment," I breathed and sailed past him, brushing against his shirtsleeve. A whiff of his fresh cologne hit my nose, and I inhaled it. He smelled yummy. I snorted as that thought hit me. I wanted nothing to do with any journalists. Ever. That could only spell trouble for me later down the line.

"I didn't even ask you anything!" Cole protested.

"You were going to," I said primly as I hustled over to my car.

He rushed after me. "You don't know that!" he said.

I rolled my eyes, but he couldn't see me. "Uh huh." I spun around. "Then why are you here and why didn't you want the police to see you?"

A chagrined smile lit his generous lips. "Maybe I just saw a pretty lady and wanted to talk to her." He took a hand out of his pocket and pulled it through his hair, messing it up even more. Cole looked rakishly adorable, and I felt myself weakening.

I stood a little straighter and chastised myself mentally. I was better than this. He was just a cute guy being cute in an effort to gain information.

An amused huff came from me. I rolled my eyes and looked down to dig in my purse for my keys. "I'm sure that's exactly what happened." Hitting the unlock button on my car, I turned and rushed over to it. The old blue Toyota Rav 4 was perfect for hauling boxes of books around but not too big to be a gas guzzler. I loved everything about it.

Cole came up beside me. "If you just have a couple of minutes..."

"I don't," I said as I opened the driver's side door.

"How about a cup of coffee?" he asked, his green eyes lit with hope.

"I don't drink coffee," I lied. Sliding into the seat, I gave him a little wave.

"Dinner!" he barked desperately.

I started the engine. "I'm on a hunger strike," I declared just before I shut the door.

His surprised shout out of laughter made me grin as I hit the gas and left him standing in the road.

FOUR

Thoughts of Marcy plagued me all the way back to the bookshop. That poor woman. I hoped that whatever happened came quickly and she didn't suffer. I shuddered as the image of her prone body kept running through my mind.

The bag with her book rested in the seat next to me, and a sigh escaped me when I glanced down at it as I sat at a red light. I would have to eat the cost of it for now. Considering the circumstances, it was a small thing. I'd lock it in the cabinet when I got back to the store.

Frowning, I wondered if the police were going to confiscate the book. I wouldn't think so, but if something came back weird, it might come up. I didn't know squat about police work, though I'd gotten an unwanted look at it today. Reaching over, I clicked the heater up a little higher. Just thinking of it was making me colder.

My life was free of drama or craziness. I liked to be

surrounded by books, coffee, and the occasional family member. Even they got on my nerves sometimes. I had a few friends I really liked, and I spent time with them when I could.

People were surprised when they found out how much time it took to run a bookstore. I wouldn't change it for the world, though. I did not have any siblings, something my mom lamented when she thought I was being a brat.

For the record, it was usually a toss-up between me and Mom as to who was being the bigger brat. Thoughts of her made me smile. Dad passed away about seven years ago after a long battle with cancer. Mom had been a trooper through the entire thing, but even I couldn't miss the shadows that still haunted her after all these years. Those two were peas in a pod. Tears swam in my eyes. I tried not to think about my dad too much. When I did, all the emotion I'd been stifling down for years pooled in my heart and I'd cry for ages.

I wondered where Marcy's family was or if she just had Carrie. I hoped she had someone who loved her like my father loved me. I didn't think Carrie cared about her in a productive or meaningful way, but I hoped I was wrong.

I blew out a slow breath and turned into the parking lot of the store. Dashing the wetness out my eyes, I sat in the car for another moment trying to calm my thoughts.

I was going to call my mom tonight, maybe take her to dinner or invite her over. I hadn't seen her in a few days. In a town as small as this, that was practically forever.

. . .

HARPER GREETED me as soon as the bell over the door sounded, but her face fell as soon as she saw me. Concern lit her eyes as she rushed over, her cool hands lightly gripping me by the upper arms.

"Dakota? What's wrong?" Her gaze raked over me as if she was looking for an injury.

I gave her a wan smile. "Marcy." I said as I dropped my bag behind the counter. I sank into the seat we kept back there for the days when we stood so long our feet ached.

"She didn't like the book?" Harper asked. Her face was so innocent that I hesitated to break the news. She'd find out soon enough, though.

"No," I said, my voice thick with tears. "She passed away. I found her."

A shocked gasp came from my friend. She swayed and reached out to grip the edge of the counter. "My goodness," she breathed. "That's terrible." Her eyes searched mine. "Are you okay?"

I nodded. "I'm okay. Just surprised. And sad." I hugged myself and rubbed my arms, trying to shake off the feeling of death.

"I wonder what happened to her?" she mused aloud. "She didn't seem well when she came in here the other day, but she also didn't seem like she was on her deathbed either."

"I know," I agreed. "I couldn't tell what happened to her. She was just lying there so still." I waved a hand. "I don't want to talk about it, if that's okay." I pulled the bag up. "I brought the book back. We'll have to try to recoup our money on it. Maybe we can list it on our Facebook page."

Harper took it from me. "Of course. I'll pop it in the safe for now." She shook her head. "That's a shame. I'm so sorry you had to see that. And that it even happened." An unhappy look crossed her face.

I nodded my thanks as Harper turned to walk to the back. Nothing was suspicious about Marcy's death, but I couldn't quite shake the feeling I was missing something.

Something important.

I KICKED off my shoes and groaned as my feet sank into the plush carpet of my living room. I'd just installed it a few weeks ago after I'd gone back and forth with myself trying to decide between wood look ceramic or carpet. In the end, I'd chosen both. I went with carpet in the living room and ceramic tile in the kitchen, foyer, utility room, bathrooms, and hallways. All the bedrooms had new carpet. There was nothing worse than waking up on a cold morning here and touching bare toes to freezing tile.

I shrugged off my jacket and settled it on the back of the old brown leather recliner that used to belong to my dad. Every time I sat in it, I caught a whiff of the Old Spice he used to use and it made me melancholy. I tried not to sit in it as much anymore for fear the smell of his would fade.

I let out a sigh and sat down on the couch. Swinging

my feet up, I laid back for a moment, staring up at the ceiling. What a day today had been. Surprisingly enough, word about what happened to Marcy had not yet connected back to me. I knew this was only a reprieve. Silverwood Hollow was a smaller town and soon enough someone was going to get wind that I'd been the one to discover her. Then I wouldn't be able to beat the gossips off of me.

I fumbled for my back pocket and pulled my cell out to call Mom. She answered on the second ring in her high, breathy voice.

"Dakota!" she said. "How nice to hear from you!"

This was Mom speak for why haven't you called me sooner? I stifled a grin. "Hi Mom. What's going on?"

"Well," she breathed, "I went to a yoga class at that new studio in the town square. The woman who owns it is insufferably rude!"

I blinked. Mom rarely said anyone was rude so the woman must have been a tyrant. "Really?"

"Yes! She told me and Irma that we couldn't talk in class!"

I chewed on my lip to keep from laughing.

"I've never been in a class where I couldn't chat to the person next to me. I'm never going back." She huffed an annoyed breath.

"Mom, yoga is different from other workouts. It's all about Zen and inner peace. The physical benefits are secondary." I eyed the stack of yoga DVD's I kept procrastinating doing because of how late I sometimes got home. I loved it, though. They looked lonely sitting on top of my white TV pedestal, unused and a little dusty. I'd need to clean this weekend before tumbleweeds started rolling across my carpet.

"What about my inner peace?" my mom whined.

A laugh escaped me. "I'm not sure yoga is your thing, mom, but it was nice that you gave it a try."

She harrumphed. "Maybe I'll go back just to spite the woman." Her voice lowered. "She's French," she whispered.

"Umm ... okay?" I shook my head as I got off the couch and padded into the kitchen.

"We don't have anyone French here!" She said it like being French was scandalous. I thought it was glamorous, and I made a note to stop by her studio to meet her. Maybe I'd even sign up for a class if I could squeeze it in.

"Diversity is the spice of life, Mom." I grabbed a glass of water and chugged it as she continued to talk.

"Well, she is awfully pretty," she said. "It won't be no time before some handsome man comes in and snatches her right up."

"Even though she's mean?" I said, unable to keep the grin out of my voice.

She had the grace to laugh. "Dakota Adair! You shouldn't make fun of your mother. What I wish would happen is for some eligible gentleman to come snatch you up. I'm not getting any younger, you know."

I rolled my eyes. "I'm not interested in anyone coming to snatch me up, Mom. I've got more than enough to keep me busy." I was serious. My biological clock was not tick-ing, and I wasn't sure if it ever would. Sure, it would be nice to settle down with someone. It did get kind of lonely in this little house. But I didn't immediately want to jump into kids. I wasn't even sure I wanted kids. When they came into the bookstore, I found them to be slightly terrifying with their sticky hands and their crazy grins.

"I'm sure you do, darling, but eventually I'd love to have some grandkids."

I changed the subject before it could escalate. At least once a month, Mom would drop the baby bomb. I didn't have the heart to tell her grandkids were not on the horizon for the foreseeable future.

"I wanted to tell you something before you heard it from anyone else." I began.

Mom quieted down and listened. She didn't interrupt and when I finished, I heard her soft exhalation over the phone. "Oh, honey, that's terrible. Do you want me to come over?"

Tears filled my eyes, but I kept the emotion out of my voice. "I'd love it if you came over for dinner tonight. I was thinking about making pasta. Does that sound good?"

She tsked. "Of course, it does. If you come over here, I can cook."

I shook my head even though she couldn't hear it. "I'd like to stay in if you don't mind. I have all the stuff to make it here."

"Okay, honey. I'll bring a loaf of bread and some wine, then. Should we say 7?"

"That sounds good, Mom. I'll see you then."

We disconnected the line and I let my shoulders fall. I was thirty-three years old, but I knew when to admit I needed my mom. I rummaged through my pantry and pulled out everything I needed to make a balsamic cream pasta. It was one of my favorite recipes, but I'd ended up making it better once I started tweaking it. I loved to cook, but it wasn't always fun cooking for one. I needed to figure out how to pare my recipes down, so I didn't end up with so many leftovers, but since Mom was coming tonight, I knew I'd have just enough left over to take to work tomorrow.

Smiling, I got out the cutting board and set it on top of the counter. From the fridge, I pulled out a shallot, a clove of garlic, and a pack of baby bella mushrooms. Once I'd finished cutting everything up, I heated a little avocado oil and a pat of butter up and started sautéing everything. A quick glance at my cell phone had me speeding up the pace a little bit. I didn't want Mom to have to wait too long when she came over. It was already six, so I was lucky I'd caught her before she ate. It seemed like the older you get, the earlier you ate and went to bed. If Mom was coming over at seven, I needed to be shoving food at her as soon as she came in so she wouldn't fall asleep at the table.

I snickered to myself as I stirred the veggies. Mom was wonderful, but she was cantankerous about her bedtime.

THE DOORBELL RANG RIGHT at seven. I took my apron off, fluffed my hair, and answered the door. Mom stood there holding a bottle of wine and an enormous baguette. I took both from her and she swept in before I even had the chance to open the door all the way.

"It smells wonderful in here! Is that the balsamic cream sauce?" She walked into the kitchen and leaned over the pan to inhale it. "I swear. That dish is the best, isn't it?"

"It really is. I had no idea how delicious vinegar was until I finally started to cook with it." I messed with the cork until I got it out of the bottle, making a mental note to buy a new wine opener as soon as I paid myself. The one I had was ancient and given to me by Mom whenever she'd gone through all of Dad's old things. I didn't drink a lot of wine, but I did drink it often enough to get a better opener.

Mom took the bread from me and started to slice it. In only a few minutes, we had bowls filled to the brim with pasta and grilled chicken and a glass full of wine.

I let her take the first bite because I liked cooking for my mom, and I knew she appreciated it. After all, she'd spent half her life cooking for me.

Everly Adair was still a beautiful woman, though the grief of my father's death had etched small lines into the corners of her eyes and mouth. She would be fifty-seven this year, though she looked to be in her mid-forties. Her hair was still dark, just like mine and her eyes still a clear glass blue. Her figure was trim and kept that way through a dogged devotion to exercise. She claimed she liked to eat and if you liked to eat, you had to like moving your body because it was the only way you wouldn't get sluggish. Mom practiced what she preached, though I didn't know if yoga would be in her repertoire anymore after the run-in with the French lady.

Mom sighed as she chewed the first bite. "You might be a better cook than me, honey," she said after she swallowed.

"Doubtful," I said, even as pink colored my cheeks. "I learned from the best."

We sat there for over an hour, drinking wine and chatting, and I realized that my mom was wonderful. I mean, I knew she was, but I'd neglected our relationship because I'd gotten caught up with the bookstore. I vowed right then and there to spend more time with her. After all, I liked my mom as a person. She was cool to hang around with and not much rattled her.

After we finished and poured one more glass of wine, Mom stood and went into the living room. "I love this carpet, Dakota. I didn't think the dark gray would work, but you've proven me wrong. It looks really good with the wall color." She peered at the walls. "What is it again?"

"It's pewter. The color changes depending on the lighting." Sometimes it looked taupe and other times it looked gray. It was one of my favorite neutral colors. The rest of the rooms in the house had gotten more color, but I wanted to keep this one an open palette so I could redecorate whenever I wanted to.

"Irma keeps bugging me to put some color on the walls," she murmured. Irma was her long-time best friend, a feisty woman with a tendency to say whatever she was thinking, no matter how inappropriate it was. She made me laugh all the time, but that was probably because I didn't see her a lot. She could really annoy Mom, but my mother loved her and so she put up with her. That wasn't to say Mom didn't drive Irma crazy too. I could see how those two would butt heads, but they worked through any issues like that and managed to still wreak havoc on Silverwood Hollow on any given day. "I don't know how I feel about some of those colors she's picking out, though." Mom made a face of distaste. "Green is so hard to gauge. Some of those just look like I splashed baby puke on the walls."

A snort escaped me. "It's your house, Mom. Make it whatever color you want."

She sat on the couch and kicked her shoes off. "That's the thing. I don't know what color I want. I just want it to be pretty. Magically." She waved her hand. "Like in five seconds. Boom. I didn't even have to break a sweat."

"If you pick out your colors, I can help you. If it's on a weekend," I added. I was too tired and grumpy to paint during the week, although I would if she absolutely needed it. "I can come over and help you choose. Just get some paint samples that you think you might like so we can narrow it down."

"I'll do that," she said. Her eyes took on a faraway look. "I was chatting with Irma about Marcy. We both vaguely knew her." Mom rolled her eyes. "Carrie was the one we knew more simply because she was kind of a nasty character, you know. Her mom used to come into the old beauty salon. You know the one on the outskirts of town?"

"Wanda's?" I asked.

Mom snapped her fingers. "That's the one. She was the

sweetest little thing. And she had those two little girls. Carrie was always *so* bossy."

I lowered the wine glass I was holding. "You knew them for that long?"

She nodded. "Oh yes. It was a terrible tragedy what happened to them."

My brow furrowed as I waited for her to continue, but Mom just took a sip of wine. "Mom!"

Mom blinked. "What, Dakota? My goodness. Sometimes you have terrible manners."

I snorted. "You can't just say something like that and not elaborate."

Her brow furrowed. "You don't know?" She clucked her tongue. "I thought everyone knew about that."

"No, Mom. I don't pay attention to much that goes on in this town." I was fibbing a little bit about that. People who came into Tattered Pages loved to gossip, so I heard almost everything going on. Most of it I forgot soon afterward now, especially since it didn't affect me.

"Their parents were killed in a car accident a few towns over. On their way to a play, I think." She shook her head, her dark hair moving against her face. "The girls were left without parents and went to stay with an aunt down the road. Terrible business that."

Curiosity made me sit up straighter. "What did their parents do?"

Mom chewed on her bottom lip. "I think the mom was a writer or something. The father was a professor down at the local college. English Lit if I'm not mistaken."

That would explain Marcy's love of reading. "She came into the shop right before she died and had me track down an Alice in Wonderland book," I said. "Marcy wasn't overly concerned about the value of it, but Carrie was. She wanted Marcy to get the most expensive collector's edition on the market."

Mom sipped her wine. She was a reader, but she wasn't as avid about it as I was. Once a week, she'd pop into the store and grab something new. She'd just joined a book club, but so far it seemed like they drank more wine than they read.

"That doesn't surprise me," Mom said. "Carrie always acted like the world owed her. Her aunt would pop by the salon sometimes with them after their mom passed away. If anything, Marcy got sweeter and Carrie got worse. That's a shame. I wonder what Carrie is going to do without her sister."

I shrugged. "They seemed joined at the hip when they were in my store."

Mom nodded her head. "They've been that way for years." She set down her wineglass and gathered her purse. "I gotta go, honey. I have a trainer coming over at 6:30 in the morning."

At my shocked look, she grinned. "I gotta keep in shape and it won't be with yoga, so I hired a guy named Dan to come rouse me out of bed in the mornings and run me around the park for a while. You should come."

At my look of horror, laughter burbled from her. "It would do you good, Dakota. You're wasting away surrounded by books when your lungs are screaming for fresh air."

"That sounds like I'd rather die," I said and stood to hug her. "Besides, I like my books."

She gathered me in her arms like she used to do when I was a kid, almost suffocating me with the fresh scent of her perfume. "People are better," she said. "And stranger than fiction sometimes." She glanced over to the kitchen. "Need any help with the dishes?" she asked.

I shook my head. "No thanks. Be careful on the way home, Mom. Text me when you get there."

She opened the door and stepped into the hallway. "I will. Try to set aside the events of today. Tomorrow is a brand new one." A grin lit her face as she turned to go.

Mom and her peppy sayings. I sighed and pushed the door shut. Getting to bed at a decent hour sounded like an amazing idea. I had a busy day tomorrow.

FIVE

The shop phone rang at five past nine. Distracted, I leaned over and reached for it, my attention still on balancing everything I was holding. If I was out of the shop, I had the phone set up to divert to my cell unless it was normal after business stuff. Most things could wait until the next day, but with everything going on, I was setting the call forwarding up whenever I left the store. At least until all of this was over.

"Dakota," I barked, annoyed that someone would be calling me when I'd just gotten into the shop.

"Miss Adair?" a rumbly, familiar voice said.

"Yes," I said, trying to balance my cup of coffee while bending my head to chat on the phone.

"This is Detective Cavanaugh. How are you this morning?"

I almost dropped my drink. Why in the world was he

calling me? "I'm ... well," I drawled, confusion dripping from my words.

A snort escaped him as if he knew what I was thinking. "Listen, I'm sorry to bother you so early in the morning, but I was wondering if you'd be able to drop by Marcy's house today. There's something I want you to look at, and my understanding is that you're the only one in town qualified to do it."

"Do what?" I asked, finally setting my coffee down. "I don't want to see anything disturbing," I said. "I had quite enough of that yesterday."

Cavanaugh chuckled. "Nothing weird, I assure you. After we went through the house, we found an enormous number of books scattered in a few of the rooms. One of my co-workers is a big reader and was astounded at some of the books the deceased had. She suggested we call in someone who might help us fully understand the value of what she had. If we have a roundabout number, it would help us in the investigation. The house is still closed off, but I can get you in if you have some time. Maybe around one today?" he concluded brightly.

I wasn't interested in going back to Marcy's house, but I'd also never been asked to assist on an investigation before and my curiosity was killing me.

"One," I agreed. "I can't be gone for more than an hour. Harper isn't here today so I have to get back to the shop."

"Great," Cavanaugh said, and I could hear the relief in his voice. "I'll swing by and get you."

Frowning, I looked at the clock across the room. I had a

few hours. "I'd rather drive myself if you don't mind. It's a small town, and I'm not really interested in answering questions about why I got into a police car."

His amused chuckle rumbled through the line. "Detectives don't drive cruisers, but I understand. I thought it might be easier for you than having your car show up at an active crime scene."

I blinked. He was right. "Err ... Fine," I said and sighed. "As long as your car doesn't look like a police car."

"It's a dark sedan, Miss Adair. I might be a detective, but I'm not a wizard. I'll keep the lights and sirens off."

"Ha. Funny," I said.

"I'll see you at one," Cavanaugh said, amusement in his voice. He hung up, and I laid my cell down, shaking my head.

This was certainly odd. Exactly how many books did this woman have to call in someone like me? After I graduated from college, I'd gone on to receive certification in rare books, simply because I had a passion for them. I'd kept up with it and it had come in handy once I opened my own shop. I was one of the few people in the entire state who was qualified, but I usually only got called in when something was worth over a few grand.

Frowning, I picked my coffee back up and took a sip. I knew Marcy had some books, but I didn't realize she had quite that many. Maybe that was what the funny smell was when I was in her house. Sometimes older books had a musty smell to them, especially if they weren't properly cared for.

Harper had taken the day off to run errands, so it was just me here. The shop opened up at ten and I rarely shut it down for anything other than lunch. Firing up my laptop, I posted a quick message on our Facebook page that I'd be gone for about an hour today, then scrawled out a quick note and taped it on the door.

People would still get annoyed by my absence because that was just the nature of the beast, but at least I'd done my part to keep people informed.

Carrying my cup, I did a quick walk around the store, taking the time to tuck books back in that might have been pulled out too far. If I saw anything amiss, I reshelved it. I straightened up the front display with the newest books we had to offer and dusted off the window display. We'd need to change it soon, especially with the colder air coming in.

A quick glance at my cell told me I'd wasted enough time. With five minutes to spare, I opened up the shop and flipped on the lights. No one was waiting outside, but I knew we'd have our first customer in just a few minutes.

The bell jangled just as I turned to walk back to the office for a quick sec. I pushed the sliver of annoyance at being interrupted down and greeted the person with a smile. It was a young woman holding the hand of a little blonde-haired girl. I waved at her and she rewarded me with a dimpled smile.

"Come on in," I said. "We've just opened so you have the place to yourself for now."

The mom smiled gratefully. "The children's section?" she asked.

I pointed toward the back. "There's a seating area back there, too."

The woman tugged the little girl's hand gently, and I watched as they walked back together. Longing pierced me right in the stomach and I sucked in a breath. I had no desire for a kiddo, especially right now, but watching that little girl put all her trust in her mom ... well, that kind of got me.

Shaking my head, I went back behind the counter and settled in for a few hours of work. I pushed down the anticipation of meeting Detective Cavanaugh. Being excited over books was fine, but the only reason I was going over there was because of something far more tragic. I needed to remember that when the excitement of the books got to me. And they would. Books had been my life ever since I was a kid. Sometimes I had to remember to pull my nose out of one and get to living.

Sometimes it was more difficult than it sounded. Books were easy.

Real life was hard.

DETECTIVE CAVANAUGH PULLED up to the front of the store five minutes early. Fortunately, he did not get out of his car, and I rushed out the door as soon as I saw him roll down his window and wave at me. I'd been standing by the door impatiently, my gloves and hat held loosely in my hands. I already had my jacket on and my purse gathered. I pulled open the door, turned to lock the shop up, and then ran down the steps like my tail was on fire. A quick glance around told me no one was watching me, but this town was so small and so prone to gossip, you never knew when someone would be peeking out from behind the blinds.

I slid into the newer model Toyota Avalon and groaned a sigh of relief at the warm air blowing through the vents. I slid my gloves on anyway because it wouldn't take too long to get to Marcy's. "This is a nice ride," I said, smiling at the detective as I buckled my seatbelt.

Clarke had taken up most of the questioning at Marcy's house, so I didn't get to fully check Cavanaugh out. I was not immune to a strong jawline and long lashes on the male species, both of which he had in spades.

His hair was dark and cropped short to his head, making his deep blue eyes stand out even more. Cavanaugh's skin was darker. If I had to peg him, I thought he might be Italian or possibly even Greek. His cheekbones were high, and his lips were generous.

I was in the car with a stunner and I hadn't even realized it.

"They just upgraded the fleet of cars, so I got lucky to slide into this one." He grimaced. "Usually we get stuck with cars that have years' worth of coffee spills in them."

"Nice," I agreed. I sat back in the comfy leather seat and adjusted the purse on my lap. "What is it exactly you want me to do?"

"I know you only have an hour, but we're trying to see if you can give us a roundabout value on the book collection she has." He drove with both hands on the wheel, in a perfect ten and two position.

"I'll do my best. I really can't promise how far I'll get, but I'll skim and see if anything jumps out at me."

His jaw clenched. "I bet it will," he murmured.

My brows drew together. "Did something happen?"

"We can't find any evidence of foul play," Cavanaugh said. He pressed his lips together.

My heart began to pound. "But you suspect there is?" I asked aloud. "Why?"

Cavanaugh clammed up and wouldn't say anything more, but a thought occurred to me. "It's the books, isn't it?" I breathed. "You think someone was after them."

He didn't confirm or deny, but I suspected I was on the right track with them. "Wow," I said. "If that's the case, that's pretty risky. There are only a certain number of serious collectors in the states," I added. "Wouldn't it be easier to just narrow those down?" I frowned. "Even if they hurt Marcy, though, they wouldn't be able to get their hands on those books. Not legally, anyway."

Cavanaugh made a smooth left turn and drove in silence. My mind spun with the implications. "You don't think this was an accident." I ran a hand over my face. "But I didn't see a speck of blood anywhere. Or anything else for that matter."

The detective sighed. "The ME is working on it. We should have initial findings in a day or two. The toxicology screens may take longer to come back."

I shook my head and turned to stare out the window.

One problem I always had was people thinking they could take your things just because they wanted whatever you had. Growing up in Virginia, I hadn't run into a lot of that, but there had been times in school when students got their way when they shouldn't have. This felt like one of those instances, but in this case, the consequences were a lot more deadly.

We fell into a companionable silence, but I snuck a glance out of the side of my eye and noticed how tight Cavanaugh's jaw was compared to the lines faintly showing at the corner of his eyes. He either knew or suspected something and it seemed like he was counting on me to make it happen.

"Cavanaugh?" I said softly.

"Hmm?" he asked, never taking his eyes off the road. His hands were white-knuckling the steering wheel. Whatever he wasn't saying was bothering him.

"If something happened to Marcy, you'll figure out what it is." I didn't know him that well, but he seemed like a trustworthy kind of guy. Plus, he was a detective. If he couldn't figure a way to make the truth come out, maybe there was no truth to be found. My mind played back to when I'd last seen Marcy, happy but a little frail browsing inside of my store. Cavanaugh looked over at me for a second before turning his gaze back to the road. "Thanks," he said softly. "There's just something ... off about it." His jaw tightened as he turned down Marcy's street.

The last time I'd been here I noticed how far apart the houses were spaced. It was a nice neighborhood, but now that I was paying more attention, I realized there were no cars in any of the driveways. That was odd for a town like this one, made up of a lot of craftsmen, artists, and retirees. I frowned as we passed by house after house and all of them looked empty.

"Do you know anything about this neighborhood?" I asked the detective.

Cavanaugh blinked as if I'd jostled him out of a memory. "Not much," he said and shrugged. "I know a lot of the houses were bought up by an investment company. The last one sold about six months ago."

Something ugly drummed in my stomach at the implications of that. He sat up a little straighter as he pulled into Marcy's driveway. As soon as he stopped the car, a contemplative look came over his face and he slid out of the vehicle with purpose.

I followed him as he walked away from her house and down the street. He stopped at the third house. This one was empty too.

Cavanaugh's jaw tightened, and he rubbed a hand over his jawline. "Good catch, Miss Adair. I'll be looking into this when I get back."

It didn't feel good. It felt like maybe he was right, and Marcy was the victim of foul play. "Do you know why they're all being purchased?" I asked. My thoughts went back to Jeff. He'd been constantly pressuring me to sell my store in an effort to just tear it down and build something for the corporate world. A conglomerate. That's the last thing this town needed.

The detective shrugged and started walking back to Marcy's. "Who knows? I always hate when investors get involved. They rarely have the good of the town in mind when they come in somewhere to snap up properties."

We walked in silence until we were on Marcy's porch. As soon as he opened the door and flipped the lights on, he started talking.

"Take as much time as you need in here. I'll be up front giving the scene another once over." He shook his head. "I don't know that I'll find much but I have to try."

I pointed down at my shoes. "Do I need to put booties on?"

"Not this time. We've done everything we need to. I'll hand the keys over to her next of kin soon."

"Is that Carrie?" I asked, not quite able to smooth out the frown forming.

His gaze sharpened as it lingered on my face. "Yes. Why? Something wrong with her?"

I hesitated to tell the detective I didn't like her. Not liking someone didn't mean they were a murderer. Shaking my head, I shrugged off my jacket. It was still chilly in here, but not like it was outside. "No. They came in my shop the other day. She was ... bossy. That's it."

But I wasn't sure that was it. Plenty of people were bossy. I'd been called bossy many times over the years. Carrie was controlling, too. Maybe more controlling than bossy.

The detective made a hmmm noise as he walked over

to where Marcy's final moments were. I sighed. Squaring my shoulders, I passed by him.

"Start at the second room on the left," Cavanaugh said, his voice distracted as he bent down to peer at something on the floor.

I passed by him, keeping a wide berth. My gaze was everywhere. The paint on the walls was a nondescript neutral, plain and beigey. There were few pictures on the wall, and none were photographs. I passed by one with a woman in a blue dress staring out the window at a beach scene. A hollow loneliness surrounded her, and my breath caught with tears as I stopped in front of the room Cavanaugh said to start in.

The door creaked and groaned as I opened it. I gasped and stepped back as that weird, sweet scent came out of the room. I put my face in the crook of my arm and stepped through. I couldn't open a window in a room full of books like this. It would allow moisture in which would decrease the value. I stumbled on my first few steps. Looking down, I noticed some of the floor had been pulled up and replaced with the new flooring. It was weird that the books were still in here if there was work being done. I reached over to flip on the light and gasped in surprise. Books, hundreds of them, lined the rooms in large wooden book-shelves. There were books stacked in piles on the floor, books in the closet, and books stacked on top of the shelves. It was like a wildly disorganized library. The bibliophile in me stood up and wanted to clap and weep all at the same time. The collector in me wanted to clutch at my hair and wail at the conditions, though.

I slowly put my arm down from my face and tried to take shallow breaths. It didn't completely diminish the sickly scent, but it helped.

I walked over to the first shelf and leaned in to examine the titles. My scalp tingled with excitement as I saw the first title. It was a copy of The Lion, The Witch and The Wardrobe. I dug around in my purse for my gloves and slid them on before I handled the title.

Cracking open the spine, the scent of must and something I couldn't identify hit me. The pages were in wonderful condition and I couldn't see any water damage. I held the book up and turned it to study it further in the light. My pulse pounded as I turned to the copyright page.

In my hands I was holding a first edition. Of Narnia. Freaking Narnia! My hands trembled as I carefully placed the book back in its place. It should be in a temperature-controlled room probably under lock and key. If I had to guess, the book was worth at least ten grand. I pulled a notepad and pen out of my purse and started to take notes. I only had an hour, but if Cavanaugh would let me, I'd try to come back and see what else she had. If that was the first book, there was no telling what she had in here.

I swallowed hard and got busy.

SIX

I flipped off the lights in the third bedroom I was in, Marcy's master by the looks of it. Slapping my thighs to rid them of the dust I'd gathered, I found Cavanaugh. He'd made a place for himself at her kitchen table, his notes and pictures spread out around him. As soon as I stepped into the room, he turned, a surprised expression on his face. "Done already?" he asked. "I thought you would have been in there for hours."

A sheepish smile lit my face. "I really do have to get back. Any other time you would have been right."

"What's the verdict?" He put his pen down and gave me all of his attention.

I shook my head, in awe at what I'd just seen. "Her collection is incredible. It should be under lock and key."

Cavanaugh's expression turned to one of anticipation. "And?"

"I didn't have time to get through everything," I admitted. "That would take me weeks. Right now, my best guesstimation is a minimum of $250."

His face fell. "That's it?" he mumbled more to himself than me. "I would have expected a lot more than that."

Realizing my mistake, I chuckled. "Two hundred and fifty," I said again. "Thousand. Two hundred fifty thousand dollars."

Cavanaugh's eyebrows rose high in surprise. "Holy smokes," he muttered. "Quarter mil. Are you sure?"

"Definitely." I'd never seen a more valuable collection in my life. "She has several first editions. Some of them signed. Whoever put this collection together knew what they were doing. It's ... incredible."

The detective sat back in his chair and tapped his pen against the tabletop. "This is interesting," he said to himself.

I hiked my purse higher on my shoulder. "I need to get back," I said. "Are you about finished?"

Cavanaugh nodded and began to gather his things up. "Just give me a sec and we'll get out of here. Thanks for doing this, Miss Adair."

"Dakota," I said, feeling old every time he called me Miss.

He shoved all the papers into his computer case. "Dakota," he repeated. A smile quirked his mouth, exposing a tiny dimple I'd failed to notice the first time I'd met him. "You can call me Hardy."

Amusement trickled through me. "Hardy?" I said, trying not to laugh. "As in the Hardy Boys?" Be still my literary beating heart.

Cavanaugh sighed. "I hear it all the time. But it's my name, and I have to live with it. It's better than my middle name, that's for sure."

Interest sparked. "Oh?" I said lightly. "And what is that?"

"It's never to be divulged," Cavanaugh said. He winked as he hauled his briefcase up and snatched his keys from the table.

I laughed as I followed him out, even though I was more curious than ever now. Hardy was a good strong name, but uncommon. I had no idea what would top that as a middle name.

THE RIDE back to the store was mostly quiet. Cavanaugh appeared deep in thought. I couldn't stop thinking about all of those books. I wondered who the next of kin was. My gut told me it was Carrie. It made my heart hurt. Would she hold on to the books just to see their value grow? That's what my intuition told me. Either that or she'd sell them right away. She didn't seem like a woman who loved things for the joy they brought. I could be wrong. Sometimes first impressions went awry, but I didn't think I was.

There was something off about Marcy's sister. It still didn't mean she would harm a family member, though.

The property situation there was also weighing on my mind. Had she held out on selling and then wound up as a casualty? Whoever the next of kin was *could* sell her house. It would free up the investor's project if hers was the only one they were waiting on.

Hardy pulled up to the curb and came to a stop. His blue eyes settled on my face. "Thank you for your assistance," he said. "Can I call you if I have any more questions about those books?"

"Of course, you can," I said, sliding out of the car. "You still have my card and you know where I work."

"I do. But I did notice you didn't give me your cell number. Just the shop number."

My hand stilled on the passenger door. "I rarely give out my cell number."

His grin was teasing. "Not even to law enforcement?" he asked.

Right now, Cavanaugh looked more like the wolf who ate Red's grandma than a law enforcement officer. I cleared my throat nervously. "I practically live at the shop," I said. "It's the best way to get me. I don't check my cell phone that often. Sometimes I set up call forwarding, depending on what's going on."

He stared at me like I was an exotic bird. "Who doesn't check their cell phone every five seconds?" he asked in amazement.

"Bookworms," I said with a grin. Quietly closing his door, I turned and sped up the steps into the safety of my shop. Only when the door shut behind me did I lean against the back of it and sigh, trying to calm my racing heart. Cavanaugh was a handsome devil. I had a strong rule about not getting involved with anyone prettier than I was.

Once my breath calmed down, I flipped the sign back to *Open* and put all the lights back on. I was only fifteen minutes late. Not as bad as I expected.

Heading over to the coffee pot, I spied the new shipment of books I'd gotten a few days ago and had yet to put up. I tucked it right next to the coffee stand and had forgotten to get to it. As soon as I freshened up the pot, I pulled the box over to me and quickly opened it with my keys.

Bending down, I pulled the extra paper from the box and saw the newest shipment of hardcovers I'd ordered from a newer publisher I'd fallen in love with. Most of them were copies of a new, sweeter romance novel with dogs and kinder heroes. I was tired of alpha men in romance. I wanted someone to wake me up with a cup of coffee and a muffin the size of my face. Not demands.

The smell of the brew filtered through the entire store and I inhaled it, bringing it deep into my lungs. I hadn't had lunch yet and today was Wednesday. One town over there was a place to get a heck of a meal. I planned to get out of the store today and grab something to eat from there. I probably shouldn't leave, but I wanted some fresh air.

ONCE I'D GOTTEN SITUATED at the table and had my napkin spread in my lap, I dug in to eat. The place was super cute, but I couldn't hope to do anything like this at Tattered Pages because of a lack of space. I would love it if people were able to come in, grab a cup of coffee and a scone or something and enjoy it inside the bookstore. I wasn't interested in opening up a restaurant or anything, but I would love to have some little nibbles. I'd thought about asking the owner of Sprinkles to provide cupcakes, but every time I started to, I'd hesitate. I couldn't bear it if frosting or fillings got on any of my books. Crumbs could easily be brushed off. Maybe I'd chat with Mom about it and see if she had any ideas. We were both really good bakers, so I knew she could help me figure it out.

I'd just taken a bite of heavenly clam chowder when I overheard two women beside me chatting. My ears perked up as soon as I heard the word "books." There was a used bookstore somewhere around here, I was pretty sure, and the woman talking appeared to be the owner.

She was on the shorter side, a little plump, and had a wonderfully friendly face. Her brown eyes gleamed with the thrill of gossip as she leaned into her friend, a thinner, pinched face blonde.

"A guy came to visit me a day ago and claimed to have all kinds of first editions." The woman rolled her eyes. "He wanted to know if I was interested in buying them, but he couldn't produce proof he had them."

Alarm trickled down my spine. First editions weren't exactly common, and our towns weren't too far apart. I leaned over. "Excuse me," I said. "I don't mean to intrude, but I overheard you talking about first edition books."

The woman's gaze flashed with annoyance, but she smiled at me. "Hello," she said, her tone guarded.

"I'm Dakota Adair. I own Tattered Pages over in Silverwood Hollow, just a little way down the road. May I ask if one of those books was a C. S. Lewis?"

Her mouth dropped open. "Well," she exclaimed. "It certainly was!"

Detective Cavanaugh might be right. It was looking more and more like Marcy was the victim of foul play.

"He said those books were going to be put up for sale and he was interested in turning a profit on them." She stuck out her hand. "I'm Harriet Tulle. I own Binders down the road. I sell used books only, but I don't often dabble in the collectables. Just a few." She fanned herself. "I don't have ten grand to plunk down on an original and neither do most of my clientele."

"The woman who owned those books passed away a little while ago. Her sister is a collector, so maybe that's where he heard it from." I shook my head. There was no accounting for taste.

"Not even cold in the grave yet!" The woman exclaimed, though her eyes were still bright. This was a woman who loved to talk.

"Do you happen to remember the man's name?" I asked. Maybe I could give it to Hardy and he could investigate it.

She shook her head. "I could probably point him out if I saw him again, but he didn't leave any contact information once I told him I wasn't the right person to sell to."

Darn. "Thanks anyway," I said. "It was a pleasure to meet you."

"You as well, Dakota." The woman smiled again and turned back to her companion.

It was terrible form to immediately seek out a buyer when the will hadn't even been settled. If I could find out more about those books and how Marcy had obtained them, maybe that would help me figure this out. She didn't seem like the kind of woman who would drop that kind of money. If I had to guess, I'd say someone gave them to her or it was some kind of inheritance and her sister was jealous.

I turned my attention back to my clam chowder, intent on eating it before it got cold. Few things were worse than cold chowder.

When I got back home, I'd give Hardy a call to see if he'd heard anything about the next of kin or a will. Not that he would have. Those kinds of things were usually handled by lawyers. But ... if there was a murder involved, maybe who got those books would have some bearing on the case.

I finished eating, put my plate away, and rushed out the door. I'd already been gone too much today and needed to write down some questions for Hardy when I got back. I knew this case was none of my business, but if it involved books, and this one did, my expertise could only help them.

I drove back to the store with a sense of purpose. It had been awhile since I'd been so excited about something. I just wish there hadn't been a crime involved.

SEVEN

I had a handwritten list of questions in my hand, and I frowned down at it as I realized how presumptuous it sounded. Hardy had no reason to give me any of the information I planned to ask for. He'd already been tight-lipped beforehand. I couldn't imagine why he'd open up now.

But now I had more information. Maybe if I dangled that like a carrot, I could get him to give me some more info. The guy asking about selling those books really bothered me. I really wish Harriet had gotten some more info from him. I could only assume he planned to undercut Carrie and try to get the books for a much cheaper price than they were worth. I didn't think she'd go for that, especially since, for all her faults, she seemed to know what she was talking about when it came to book values.

I dialed the detective's number from my cell and chewed the edge of my thumb in nervousness.

"Cavanaugh," he barked into the line

"This is Dakota," I said. "I have some information for you."

"Dakota!" His voice warmed with what seemed like genuine pleasure. A flush came over me. "Give me a sec and I'll grab a notepad."

The sound of papers shuffling came through the line. "Okay. What do you have?"

"I was across town eating lunch and overheard this woman talking about a man who came into her shop looking to sell used books. She said the man claimed they were extremely rare."

Hardy's office was so quiet I could hear the pen scratching across the paper. "Let me guess. These were Marcy's books?"

"Yup. I can only assume Carrie believes she's the next to inherit those books and is already looking to sell them."

Hardy sighed over the line. "Let's not jump to conclusions. There's no evidence Carrie is set to inherit and we're still looking into the property angle. Do you have information for the guy who came in?"

I bristled with annoyance. It didn't seem like a giant leap to assume Carrie was the one who contacted the guy to sell those books. Who else would have known about them?

"So, Carrie isn't set to inherit?" I inquired. "That's an awful lot of money and Marcy didn't have any children."

"Maybe she left it to a charity," Hardy said, dodging the question.

"Do you know the name of the investment company

who bought up all those houses?" I asked, scratching off the inheritance question from my list. If he'd avoided the question twice now, he wasn't going to answer it.

A sigh escaped him. "Dakota, I can't give you any of the information you're asking for. This is an active police investigation and all of this information is sensitive."

I huffed. "Even though I helped?"

"Especially because you helped. I didn't exactly get that cleared through the right channels."

Dakota heard the sound of shuffling. What in the world was he doing? Erasing the lead she'd just given him?

"I appreciate you calling me with this, and I promise we'll check it out."

I rolled my eyes. "You're welcome," I said, though I sounded sullen. "Look," I said after a moment once I realized how I sounded. "I'm just trying to help."

"I know you are. But it's time to let us do our job." His voice was gentle, but I still felt dismissed.

Hurt, I swallowed hard. "Any time," I said before I hung up. I didn't wait for him to say goodbye. I slapped my cell phone down on the counter and groaned with relief when I realized it was closing time. I got off the seat, grabbed my belongings, and did a quick walk-through of the shop to make sure I'd unplugged the coffee machine and nothing was too out of place.

When I came back to the counter, I realized I forgot to cash out the register. I blew out a breath, set everything down and took care of that.

Twenty minutes later, I nudged Poppy with a toe and

called for her to hop up on the counter so I could grab her before I locked up the store and set off home. When I stepped out of the store, I hugged Poppy and tugged my jacket closer around me. It was positively freezing this evening!

I gently set Poppy in the front seat as she voiced her displeasure. Snorting with amusement, I hurried around to the other side of the car so I could turn the heater on. In the past, I would put Poppy in a carrier and drive her home that way. One day she abruptly decided she wanted absolutely nothing to do with a carrier anymore and would fight me tooth and claw when I would try to put her in one. I let her ride without it in the car for short drives and since she ended up doing just fine, I'd installed a cat hammock in the back. Most of the time she chose to ride in that, even though I looked ridiculous driving around town with a cat lounging in the back without a care in the world. Some days when it got too cold, she'd choose to ride in the front seat with me, yowling until I got the air vents to point at her just right. Then she'd soak up all the heat and curl in the front seat, content with me doing all the work.

"You're a mess, cat," I said as I started the vehicle and cranked up the heat. She turned her head as if to say, "So," before she faced the vents again.

I chuckled as I pulled out of my space. I never wanted a cat, but I'm grateful she came along.

Even if she was high maintenance.

. . .

I DISHED Poppy out her food, her voicing her displeasure the entire time. I'd never seen a noisier cat. She could creep up to you and scare the mess out of you, but on days like today I couldn't seem to keep her quiet. When I finally set the dish down, her tail went straight up, and she sashayed to it like she hadn't just made a fool of herself two seconds prior.

"Uh huh. You little drama queen," I muttered.

I was streaming indie folk through my Bluetooth speaker. Harper was due over any second. We had to discuss the upcoming festival, and we were already behind. I was still leaning toward just pies, but people would really want something to drink, too. It would be a good chance for me to check out some offerings from the store.

The doorbell rang just as I was putting the final touches on the cheese and cracker tray. Harper and I never had a meeting or get together when there weren't any crackers and cheese. Over the months, the trays had gotten more and more elaborate with the selection. Tonight, I had gluten-free smoked paprika nut crackers, rice crackers, and buttermilk ranch pita crisps with Havarti, Smoked Gouda, and Irish Cheddar. A bottle of wine was open and breathing on the dining room table.

"Coming!" I called and rushed over to the door.

Harper stood there; her cheeks flushed from the cold weather. "Hey!" she chirped and held up a wine bottle like a trophy. "I brought sustenance!" she said and walked into the apartment.

"I have real sustenance," I said and pointed over to the tray.

"Ooh." Harper's fingers moved into claws. "Gimme." She unwound her scarf and unbuttoned her jacket, tossing it up on the stand by the door before she rushed over to fill a plate. I smiled as I poured her a glass of Malbec.

She moaned as she took a bite of the smoked Gouda. "Oh my word. What is this?" She peered down at the tray. "I know you didn't get that down at the town grocery store." Her green eyes glittered with envy as she looked up at me. "You little cheat," she accused with no heat. We'd previously agreed to eat cheese only bought from Shaw's as a way to save money.

"I couldn't help it," I said. "I have a cheese problem."

"Well, maybe we could bend the rules a little bit," she said, picking up another piece. "As long as I can have some more of the gouda."

"Deal," I said and poured myself a glass of wine, too. I motioned for her to sit down.

Pulling my pad and paper over, I took a sip and wrote Harvest Festival at the top of the paper. "I'm still thinking pies only. I can't decide if we should do drinks, too."

Harper crunched into one of the nut crackers and chewed, a thoughtful look on her face. "I think it would be cool. No one has ever had a drink contest. Maybe we could do hot only because it's going to be pretty cool out there, especially for the tourists, depending on where they're from."

I nodded. "I like that idea. Fall drinks only, must be

hot. We'll have to make sure we have plenty of plugs for the inevitable crockpot set up."

"I can take that on," she volunteered. "Don't forget the best use of cinnamon and cloves. We can open that up to either category."

I glanced up. "Are you going to make something?"

Her eyes sparkled with amusement. "I can't win," she pouted, "but I still might make something just to keep at the table."

I tapped my pen on the table as a smile curled onto my lips. "Please, please, please make that mulled wine recipe. It's to die for."

A dimple peeked out from her cheek. "I think I could do that. But you have to promise not to let Corky get into it again."

Last year Harper brought her mulled wine to the bookstore for a harvest event. My aunt had found her thermos, gotten into it, and proceeded to have a dance off in the main area of Tattered Pages. The only reason I'd let it go is because everyone was having so much fun. "Maybe we can put a lock on your thermos?" I suggested.

Harper laughed, a merry sound. "Maybe we should just make sure it doesn't get out of our sight. I'm sure Corky will find a way, though."

I'm sure she would. The entire town loved her, but her antics were sometimes out of control. No one was ever harmed, but I found Aunt Corky exhausting sometimes. Mom grew up with the woman, so all she did was sigh and roll her eyes when things got especially outrageous.

I scratched a couple more ideas on to the paper, but I paused when a thought occurred to me. "Harper, have you heard anything about anyone selling any rare books?" The odds were low especially since the man went to the town over to try to sell them, but you never knew what you might overhear in a town this size.

She shook her head. "Not that, but I did overhear Jeff saying something really weird the other day. I stopped into the bank down the road and Jeff was there. He was talking to one of the loan officers, I think, and I heard the name of Marcy's street come up. Whatever they were talking about did not sound good. Jeff was furious."

My heart was pounding. That no good little weasel. If he was the one responsible for what happened to Marcy, regardless of if he wasn't directly responsible, I was going to fry him up for dinner and put him on top of my chowder.

"Jeff huh?" A breath of frustrated air escaped me. "Why am I not surprised?" I grumbled.

"What's going on?" Harper nibbled on another cracker as she waited.

"Some investors bought all the houses on Marcy's street. Apparently, she was the only holdout."

Harper's mouth dropped, but fortunately she'd swallowed her cracker. "You think Jeff might be involved?"

"If he was involved in trying to get her to sell, then yes, I definitely think he might be involved." I scooped a few pieces of cheese onto my plate and nibbled on one as my thoughts spun furiously. I didn't like Jeff, but I sometimes found him tolerable. I knew he was just trying to do a job, but it was a job that wasn't town friendly. He wasn't a well-liked person around Silverwood Hollow, but he hadn't made an effort either. Mostly he was all give me your property without even trying to form a relationship with anyone.

If he slowed down some and got to know us, maybe he would even like the town and the people in it. I hoped he wasn't involved. It would crush his family. His mom was a saint who came into Tattered Pages at least twice a week. I had no idea how she put up with him for all those years. Maybe this was one of those things where he was a completely different person around his family.

I hoped for his sake he was because I couldn't imagine going through life when everyone disliked you.

"That would be a shame," she said. Her face lit up. "Oh! I forgot to tell you. I ran into Jeff's brother today. He'd just gotten to town today and Jeff was trying to hurry him along, but he was stopping at all the window displays in awe." A smile quirked her lips. "He seems like a nice guy," she said. "Way unlike his brother."

I laughed at that. "Maybe he'll soften Jeff up some. Give him a personality."

Harper shuddered. "I don't know. Jeff has never been especially nice to me. If he started all of a sudden, I'd be suspicious."

"He isn't nice to anyone," I agreed. I chewed on a piece of Irish cheddar, delighting in the bite of salt on my tongue as I bit down. The Irish knew their dairy, that was for sure.

"I heard his brother is starting his first shift at the library next week," Harper said, her voice sly.

My head came up sharply at her teasing tone. "No," I said. "Do not try to play matchmaker. It will end terribly for everyone."

"Oh, come on, Dakota," Harper wheedled. Her hands clasped in front of her chest. "He is so cute! All dark haired and nerdy." She practically swooned. "His hair is just a touch too long, and he's got this five o'clock shadow." She batted her eyelashes. "He's super dreamy."

I shook my head. "I don't care if he's a rich supermodel and thinks I'm his soulmate. I'm not interested." I took a sip of my wine. "Plus, you can't have two bookworms in one home cohabitating. That's a cleaning disaster waiting to happen."

Harper snorted as she looked around my house. "Please. Your house is spotless."

"I know." I glared at her. "And I want to keep it that way. I clean it because I have to. I've never known a man good at the distribution of chores."

"That's because they take care of all the manly stuff," Harper claimed. She grinned at me.

"Like taking out the trash?" I offered. "I do that already."

"Like killing spiders." Harper shuddered. "I'd love to have a boyfriend who kills the creepy crawly things for me."

"It's going to be so cold here soon you won't have to

worry about that until at least spring." I topped off my wine glass and waved the bottle at her. She declined.

"Still. Someone to keep me warm during the winter would be nice, too."

I snorted at that. "This is Virginia. We have big jackets and even bigger blankets."

"Oh Dakota," Harper chided. "I wouldn't mind someone. I just have a particular list." Her eyes were downcast. "That no one will probably ever meet."

"I'm addicted to book boyfriends," I admitted. "No one will ever come close to measuring up to one of those."

"True," Harper said with a sigh. "Book boyfriends are the best."

I picked up my pen and tapped it. "We have to focus on this or it's going to pass us right on by. Let's make a list of people who wouldn't mind donating tables and such."

Harper grinned, though I knew she wasn't fooled by me wanting to change the subject. I had to go to the library all the time. Well ... maybe didn't have to. I wanted to. I got a lot of the books I wanted being the owner of a store, but if I wanted something special and I didn't have it, I tended to go to the library to save some money. I certainly wasn't interested in hitting up the local librarian for a date.

Silverwood Hollow was a small town. He was going to have to practically beat the women off of him, anyway. I wouldn't stand a chance with him even if I wanted it.

The thought bothered me more than I liked to admit. I thought I was passably attractive, but I didn't have anything on some of the socialites living around here.

Women close to ten years younger than me and made up to the nines. I liked scarves, boots, and hats. Wearing heels all the time did not appeal to me at all. Nor did a face full of makeup or showing up constantly at social functions. The men in this town could have those girls if they wanted them. I wanted warm clothes, a hot drink, and a ton of books around me.

That was all.

So why wasn't that weird feeling going away then?

EIGHT

A week later, I found Jeff standing in front of my store at ten sharp. I grumbled to myself as I scooped Poppy out of the seat and walked up to the front.

"I don't have time for this," I said as I unlocked the door. Poppy gave Jeff a half-hearted hiss before she went limp in my arms.

Jeff scoffed. "Time for a paying customer, you mean? I can't wait to put that on your Facebook page when I give you zero stars."

I flipped on the lights as he trailed behind me. "I've only seen you buy one thing since you've been visiting and that was just a couple of days ago. Are pigs flying? Are you actually here to buy something else?"

At his eager look, I clarified. "Besides my shop?"

Poppy leapt out of my arms with little fanfare and skidded around the corner. It could be seconds or hours until I saw her again.

"Your cat is weird," Jeff remarked.

"She doesn't like you," I said as I went around the counter and put my belongings underneath it.

"The feeling is mutual." He looked around the shop, his gaze missing nothing.

"Are you here for a book then? If you aren't, I have a lot to do today so I'm sure you can see yourself out."

"My brother is here," Jeff said.

When he didn't say anything else, I raised my eyebrows and put my hands on my hips. "So?"

"He wants to meet you." Jeff fidgeted, his feet shuffling over the carpet.

A grin formed on my face. "And so, he sent you here as his errand boy?"

"No," he snapped. "He picked up a shift today and sent me to ask you if you'd drop by the library. I guess he didn't want to make a personal call on his first day."

"A personal call?" That didn't sound right.

"You know what I mean. He didn't want to use the phone. So here I am." Jeff walked over to my new releases display and began to touch everything. I wasn't sure the man knew how to remain still. "He mentioned something about a bunch of books donated that he already has copies of."

I decided to take mercy on him. "If I have time, I'll stop by." While I had him here though ... "Do you know Marcy and Carrie?" I rubbed the side of my eye as I tried to remember their last name. I didn't think the police told me. "I can't remember their last name, but they live on Spruce."

Jeff's gaze narrowed. "I do," he said slowly. "Why?"

"I'm sure you've heard what happened to Marcy. I heard their entire street was bought up by investors."

His face went blank which told me I might be onto something. "Don't you think it's a reach for it to be a coincidence that Marcy died right after she refused to sell to those people again?"

His stare was cold. Jeff wasn't a bad looking guy, but his personality was so terrible that it made him unattractive to me. Occasionally I'd seen bright spots in him, but today it was like looking at an arctic storm. His brown eyes were on the lighter side, more hazel if I had to guess. His face was ruggedly handsome with a strong jaw line and a straight, patrician nose. He had a great smile if he ever used it. Around me it was almost non-existent. Dark hair was clipped and styled, and I'd never seen it mussed, even when the day was really windy, not uncommon around here.

"That sounds like a question for the police." Jeff tugged his jacket closer. "Are you going to visit my brother?" he asked.

I shrugged. "I'll try." It was a non-answer and we both knew it. "Were you involved in the investment deal?"

Jeff sighed. "These questions you're asking ... they're going to get you into trouble."

"You didn't answer my question." My hands gripped the edge of the counter tightly as I waited for him to admit he was involved.

He slowly shook his head. "I'm not involved with the

investment company." His mouth turned down. "I asked Marcy to sell to me twice and she refused. The investment company came in and offered more money than I could for those houses." He snorted. "They want to develop the land over there and put in an upscale strip mall."

I nodded slowly. "And what did you want to do with it?" I didn't want Jeff to suddenly feel like he was a hero or something for getting outbid. The odds were good he wanted to do something similar.

"New houses," Jeff said. "The ones on that road are all in a state of disrepair. If not on the outside, then the inside. I figured I could put up some pretty beach houses there." Jeff shrugged. When he saw my surprise, a small smile lit his face. "I'm not a total monster."

Hmm. Maybe not. But he should still be considered a suspect considering he was trying to pressure Marcy to sell. If she ended up selling to him and not the investors, Jeff could have made a lot more money, too.

"I suppose not," I agreed, but I wasn't sure. Jeff was an opportunist, and I had a hard time liking those kinds of people.

He shook his head knowing I didn't believe him. "My job here is done." But before he went out the door, he stopped. "Is Harper due in today?"

"Umm. Yes."

He nodded and walked out. Huh. Wonder what was up with that.

. . .

THE WOMAN in question breezed into the shop about half an hour later. "Hey, Dakota!" she called as she pushed the door open with her hip. In her hand was a drink container holding two large coffees from down the street.

"You're a lifesaver," I said as I rushed over to help her.

I took the drink container and held the door as she struggled with her shoulder bag and a canvas bag. "Are you moving in? I asked her.

"Hardly," she said, "though this would be a good place to live if I ever needed it." She sat the bag down on the counter. "These are books my book club donated. There's some really good ones in here, so whatever you can't sell, I'll see if the library wants."

"Cool." I walked over to paw through the bag. There were some brand-new bestsellers in there and I could definitely use those. I set my coffee cup down and pulled out all of them to take a quick look. I'd done inventory here so often I knew almost every book we had by heart.

"Hey," I said to Harper as she got situated for the day. "Jeff was in here earlier. He was asking if you worked today."

I glanced up and noticed her cheeks were flushed with color when they weren't a second ago. "Harper?"

She met my eyes and looked away, her fingers twisting in her hands nervously. I gasped in surprise. "Oh my goodness. Harper! Are you and Jeff ...?" I swallowed hard. "Dating?"

She blinked. "No!" Harper shook her head. "No," she repeated. "He did ask me out."

My eyebrows went up to my hairline. "Jeff asked you out?"

She nodded, her cheeks still bright red. "I haven't given him an answer yet."

I walked over and sank into a seat. "It seems like you're leaning toward yes." Harper was available, gorgeous, and highly intelligent.

She didn't say anything. I blew out a breath. "Help me understand this. Don't we hate him?"

A snort came from her. "I ran into him two towns over at their Italian Festival. He was by himself and so was I." One shoulder lifted in a shrug. "We decided to walk around together." She fidgeted with her fingers. "He was pretty nice," she said softly.

I held up my hands. "Okay," I said. I couldn't believe it. "Does this mean we forgive him for pressuring me to sell this place?"

"Absolutely not," she said as she twisted her coffee cup out of the holder. "I remain staunch in my defense of Tattered Pages." A dimple peeked out as she smiled. "Maybe if I do decide to go out with him, he'd chill out about this place."

Hope flared in me for a second but died a quick death. "Oh Harper, you don't have to worry about that. I'll be fine. You date Jeff if you want to." I made a zipping motion against my lips. "I'll never say a word, and I'll never judge. I promise."

"Good." Harper exhaled deeply. "I still haven't made my mind up, though. Tell me about what's happening with

Marcy. Anything new?" She turned and grinned at me. "I'm sure you grilled Jeff alive over it when he was here."

I nodded. "Of course, I did. He claims he had nothing to do with it. I believe him. It doesn't completely exonerate him, though. He was still going over there to try to get her to sell. The investment company just beat him to it."

"But Marcy didn't sell to anyone, did she?" Harper took the lid off her coffee and blew on it.

"No. That company overbid Jeff and bought up the entire street. She was the only holdout."

"Hmmm. That looks bad," she agreed.

"It really does. Jeff is caught up in it whether he wants to be or not."

"It's looking more and more like murder, isn't it?" Harper asked sadly.

"Unfortunately. I couldn't get any info from Detective Cavanaugh." I told Harper about the man looking to sell Marcy's books in the town over. Her jaw dropped with surprise.

"Poor woman," she murmured. "She had two things people would kill to have. I guess they need to figure out which one it was."

"The land was more valuable than the books at the end of the day. Especially if the investors were looking to build on it. Carrie is most likely her next of kin and the one who would inherit the house. Maybe she cut some kind of deal with the investors."

"Her own sister?" Harper shook her head. "That's terrible. Let's hope not."

I stood up and stretched. "I hope not, too. I'm going to walk around and see if we can get some donations for the Harvest Fest. You okay here for a while?"

Harper saluted me with her mug. "Absolutely."

"Good." I grabbed my jacket and scarf off the hook. Poppy came running out from behind one of the shelves and twined around my legs. I reached down to give her a good scratch behind her ears. "She hissed at Jeff this morning," I said to Harper as I opened the door.

"Bad kitty," Harper said without any heat.

Grinning, I shrugged on my coat and walked into the cupcake shop next door. It was a little too early for cake, so that meant Trudy should have some time to talk. I stopped in front of her store and inhaled deeply. The cool crisp air combined with the smell of freshly baked cake, vanilla, and the smell of fall spices. Walking in, I raised a hand as Trudy looked up.

"Hi!" I called.

Her face split into a smile. She brushed flour off her hands and came out from behind the counter to give me a hug. I inhaled her spicy perfume and returned her grip. Trudy was an enthusiastic, wonderful hugger.

"I haven't seen you in a few days!" she said, her eyes sparkling with good humor. She was one of my favorite humans. Sweet, giving, funny, and she made delicious cupcakes. Her expression sobered. "I heard about what happened to that poor, poor woman. Nasty business, that."

"I hope they find out what happened soon," I said. "But, I'm here for a different reason. We're planning the Harvest

Fest and we're a little behind. I was wondering if you'd like to maybe donate some paper plates or cups or ... anything?" I wiggled my eyebrows which made her laugh.

"Sure, honey. Put me down for the paper plates. You're having a baking contest this year?"

I nodded, and she gave a little excited dance. "Tell me about it. What's the dessert?"

"Fall pies and drinks," I said. I looked around her shop and sighed. She always did everything so gorgeously. "Your store looks great."

Her display was full of fall baked goods. The cupcakes were the staple and lined up neatly, but in honor of the season, she'd stocked pumpkin scones, pumpkin pies, spice cakes, all the things I loved. She'd strung fall decor from the ceiling, pretty orange lights and brown acorns. The windows were decorated with fall leaves, pumpkins, gourds, and cornucopia with cookies spilling out. The tables were spread out and decorated with orange tea lights.

"Thanks," she said, flushing with pleasure. "My daughter and I came in early yesterday to get it all done." She untied her apron and took it off. "Would you like to try a new coffee recipe?" She rolled her eyes. "It's been a nightmare to get exactly right, but I'm really close. It's the newest batch."

"Sure. What is it?" I was a sucker for coffee of any kind.

"Pumpkin spice, but there's no syrup in it. I'm trying to blend pumpkin puree and spices to make a thick, fall drink."

Intrigued, I nodded eagerly. "Yes, please! That sounds awesome."

"Great." Trudy walked to the back as I sank into a seat at one of the tables. I quickly checked my phone before I stuck it back in my pocket.

A few minutes later, Trudy came back and handed me a mug brimming with cinnamon, chocolate shavings and whipped cream. "Holy moly." I took the mug and set it down carefully. "Stir or no?"

"Up to you. I'd dip the spoon in and scoop up some of the coffee with the whipped cream." Trudy took a sip and her eyes lit up. "Oh man. This might be the best yet."

I took a spoon from the table and carefully dipped it in. I made sure I got a little of the coffee and everything in one spoonful. As soon as it hit my mouth, I knew she had a winner. "Oh. My. Gosh," I said. "This is amazing. You have to enter this into the contest. I know you'll win." The drink was slightly thicker, almost like a homemade hot chocolate. The pumpkin flavor was profound, but it wasn't artificial. It was well spiced. I could taste cinnamon, cloves, nutmeg and ... "Black pepper?" I questioned.

"Yep," Trudy proclaimed proudly. "For a little heat and to bring all the flavor together."

"This is really amazing," I said. "I'd hold this recipe close to the vest. Tell no one."

"I plan on it." She winked at me. "Our secret?" Trudy held up her mug, and I clinked mine against it.

"As long as I can have a to-go mug of it."

She snorted. "Of course."

I took another sip and wanted to moan at how delicious it was. There was pumpkin spice and then there was ... this. Whatever this was. It was fall encapsulated in a small, decadent drink.

I loved this time of year in this town, and I loved people like Trudy. They kept this place breathing with art and culture.

I stuck around for a while to finish my mug and make sure she handed over the to-go cup she promised me. If Trudy didn't win the drink contest at the festival, I'd eat my scarf.

NINE

I spent two hours walking up and down the streets to the shops in the middle of town and by the time I finished, I had volunteers for just about everything we needed to put on the festival. I could donate all the plastic cups and warmers for all the drinks we needed. One of my mom's friends had a catering company, and I knew she'd let us borrow them.

I was just about to walk into my shop when a familiar blond head came around the corner.

Cole Gardener. His face lit up when he saw me, but his expression faltered when he noticed my sour expression. I walked into the shop without greeting him and seriously considered locking the door.

"Harper!" I called.

She came out of the back, alarmed. "Dakota? Everything okay?"

I exhaled heavily. "We're about to have a journalist in here. Give him nothing about anything, okay?"

Harper blinked. She was holding several paperbacks in her arms. "Okay," she said. "Why is he here?"

"He showed up at Marcy's house and wanted information." I shrugged off my jacket and hung it back up. I kept the scarf twined around my neck because I was still really cold. "I didn't tell him anything, but those guys never give up. Maybe if he gets it from you too, he'll stop coming around."

The bell jingled over the door from behind me. I gave her a meaningful look and spun around.

Cole stood there, his nose adorably red. He wore a dark green scarf with a charcoal gray jacket. His expression was adorably hurt. "You didn't even say hi!" he accused.

"Because I bet you aren't here to buy a book, are you? You're here to pump me for information." I lowered my voice, even though I didn't think anyone else was in the store right now. It was right after lunch and we usually slowed way down around then.

Cole had the grace to look guilty and even that looked cute on him. "I'm just trying to do my job," he grumbled.

"And I'm trying to do mine. Which is not give you answers to anything. I don't want to be involved in this, Mr. Gardener. I'm just a bookshop owner. That's all. There's nothing interesting about me."

His intense eyes darkened. "I don't know that I'd go that far," he said quietly. "Won't you at least let me buy you a cup of coffee?"

Harper stepped up beside me. "She'd love that!" she chirped. "Dakota loooooves coffee. All kinds. All day. Any time."

I gave her a horrified look. In turn, she gave me a smile that looked like a chipmunk hopped up on amphetamines. Her eyes were bright and crazy. "Right, Dakota?" she chirped. "Don't you love coffee?"

One of Cole's eyebrows rose. His lips quirked up in a small smile.

"I -"

Harper gave me a small shove. "I've got everything under control. Go have a cup and when you get back, we can chat some more about the Harvest Fest." Harper leaned forward and dropped her voice to a conspiratorial whisper. "Dakota loves to plan things. She's so organized and efficient."

Cole blinked.

"I am so sorry," I began.

Harper nudged me again. I stumbled forward. Cole choked down a laugh. He held his arm out to me. Sighing, I took it and allowed him to lead me out. He snagged my jacket from the hook. As he was opening the door, I turned back and mouthed, "I am going to murder you," to Harper.

Scared to death, she gave me a jaunty wave and a wink. Somehow, I'd lost control, and I didn't like it.

THE LAST THING I wanted was another cup of coffee. The pumpkin coffee Trudy had given me was still in a cup on the counter, but I begrudgingly walked with Cole. The air was frigid and fresh, making the tip of my nose cold and forcing me to put my hands in my pockets. I'd forgotten my gloves in the store.

"Sorry about that," Cole said.

An unladylike snort escaped me. "I don't think you could have stopped that hurricane even if you tried." I glanced over at him, trying to be casual. He really was cute in a geeky smart way. I wondered if he wore contacts. Was he wearing glasses now in an effort to be more endearing to the bookstore owner? I wouldn't put anything past a journalist. Silverwood Hollow thrived on gossip and it was a journalist's job to find it.

"I'm not here to trick you," Cole said, a grin teasing the edges of his mouth. "Will you relax?"

"No," I grumbled. "I'm not going to give you anything."

We stopped at the entrance to Coco's Coffee, a trendy little coffee shop that specialized in flavored blends. I couldn't help but think this shop was going to be super jealous when they realized the gem Trudy had just created in her kitchen. Cole opened the door for me and gestured for me to go in. I murmured my thanks and stepped into the scent of heavenly java and hazelnut.

"Mmm," I couldn't help but say.

"I agree." Cole unwound the scarf from his neck and led the way to the back of the shop. There was a small gathering of circular tables, far enough away from each other to have a private conversation as long as you kept your voice low. He pulled my chair out, a point in his favor, and tossed his jacket down on the opposite seat. "What would you like?"

"Just a regular coffee," I said. I hoped to not be here too long.

His eyes flashed. "Cream or sugar?"

I shook my head. "Thanks."

He ducked his head and walked back up to the counter. I tugged my scarf to make it a little looser but didn't bother to take my coat off. The sounds of the espresso machines whirred in the background. Indie folk music played through the speakers scattered around the store and the sound of murmuring voices made it really easy to relax here. The shop carried cupcakes from Sprinkles and a wide variety of quick breads. I'd had their pumpkin bread before, and it was divine. I craned my neck over to see what they had today and noticed a Cinnamon Spice bread I hadn't seen yet. Making a mental note to come back and check it out, I turned back around and put my head in my hands.

I couldn't believe Harper shoved me out like that. She'd never acted so strangely, especially not around a cute guy. Cole's face swam in my brain. He *was* super cute. The absolute last thing I needed was a journalist hanging around me, though. I liked a quiet life.

Cole came up behind me and set a mug down in front of me. He squeezed past and settled himself in the other seat.

"So," Cole said, "tell me everything you know about Marcy."

I inhaled to give him a piece of my mind, but he laughed and waved his hand. "I'm kidding, Miss Adair. Please. Let's just enjoy our coffee."

"Dakota," I corrected automatically.

"Good," he said, his eyes crinkling adorably at the edges. "This is how we converse like normal people."

A laugh escaped me. "I'm not against conversing. I just don't want to talk about Marcy."

"I gathered," he said, his tone dry as dust. "It's my job to find out all the facts, though."

"Then I'm sure the police can tell you what you want to know." They wouldn't tell him anything, but I wasn't going to say a word about that.

"Uh huh. I'm sure they've told you lots, too." Cole leaned forward. There was a glint in his green eyes I didn't like. "If we work together, I'm sure we can figure out what actually happened to Marcy before they do."

He was trying to catch me in a fib. I felt it in my gut. "Who said anything happened to Marcy?" I shook my head. "They think it's natural causes."

Cole's lips thinned. "Nice try. We both know she had a lot of value in that land. I heard she also had a good chunk of change wrapped up in books." He smiled like a shark. "Which is where you come in, of course. Word is, you were there to appraise books she had."

"Word from who?" I questioned.

"Come on Dakota. Why else would you be there?"

I sipped my coffee and studied him. What made a guy

like him tick? Money? Power? Cold, poorly made coffee and low job satisfaction?

"What makes you so sure something happened to her?" I asked instead. "She was in ill health and had been for a while."

He looked down at his cup, but not so quickly I couldn't see the gleam of interest in his eyes. "Did she tell you why she was sick?"

"Nope," I said. "The only thing she said is that she finally felt well enough to visit my shop." I sighed. "That is all you're going to get out of me today, Mr. Gardener."

"Cole, please." He turned on his all-American boy charm and I felt myself weaken just a little. I straightened up to my full height, and even though I still had to crane my neck up to look at him, I still felt like it had given me some resolve.

"Cole," I agreed. "How long have you been in town?" I'd never seen him before, not even at the many festivals we held here.

He shifted in his seat; his gaze wary. "About four months. Why?"

"I've never seen you around. Don't you think that's weird? A reporter I've never seen suddenly snooping in a small-town murder investigation?"

He sat up straighter and grinned, a devilish thing on his face. I blanched, knowing immediately what I'd done.

"Murder, you say?" Cole asked. He reached into his jacket pocket and pulled out a pen and a small notepad. "On whose authority did you say this come from?"

I wanted to punch him right in his tanned face. "No one's authority," I said. "It was a slip of the tongue. You're welcome to call the police department. It isn't a murder investigation." The lady doth protest too much, I thought, suppressing a sigh.

He wrote something on his paper and concealed it, too fast for me to see what it was. "You think it should be, though?"

"I'm not saying another word, Cole." This guy might be cute, but he was a real pain in my knickers. Picking up my mug, I held it up. "Thanks for the coffee." I snatched my jacket with my other hand, spun, and made my way out of the shop, not even stopping when I heard him call my name.

Annoyance made my steps quick and sure, and within a few minutes I was back in my shop. Cole stopped following me after the third time he called my name and I didn't turn around.

What a jerk.

Harper's eyes widened when I rushed into the shop. I saved a special glare for her before I once again took off my winter wear. "If I have to put my jacket on one more time before I go home today, I'm going to scream," I muttered under my breath as I walked inside. The bell jangled behind me, but I didn't turn around. It was probably one of the regulars.

Harper shrank under my glare. "Sorry," she said quietly. "He was so cute, though. He looked like Dakota candy."

A bark of laughter escaped me. "Dakota is on a diet," I declared. "And he might look like candy, but he's one of those onions disguised as a candy apple. Delicious on the outside. Super gross on the inside."

"Gross, am I? Ouch," came an amused voice.

Harper's eyes widened, and I spun around only to see Cole there, a wide grin on his face. I thought he'd stopped following me!

He hadn't bothered to put his jacket back on, but he didn't look cold. A white Henley shirt emphasized his lean build and made his eyes all the more green. "I just came in to apologize." A smirk tilted his mouth up. "Though I can see you're still angry. Rightfully so. What can I say? I'm a journalist at heart. I hope you'll let me buy you another cup of coffee, no strings attached." He offered a tight smile and walked out of the door.

"Le swoon," Harper said.

"Nope." I held a hand up and walked to the back. I was done with all of these men in this town. Insufferable. The lot of them.

I had two hours until the shop closed. "I'm doing inventory!" I called back to Harper. She could handle the customers for that little stunt she'd pulled with Cole earlier.

As soon as I got to the back, I sank down into my chair and groaned.

What a day.

TEN

At noon the next day, I was straightening up some books in the children's area when Harper gasped in surprise. The thing about a bookstore is nine times out of ten it's super quiet. I rushed to the front only to see Carrie, Marcy's sister standing there glaring at my assistant.

"Hello," I said politely. "Can I help you?"

Carrie was taller and thinner than Marcy had been. Her face had a perpetually pinched look to it. I could imagine if she smiled, she'd still look unhappy. "I'm here for the book my sister ordered."

I had it locked up in the back. "Oh good! I'll go get it." I gave her a small smile. "I wasn't sure what to do with after what happened. Please accept my condolences on your loss."

Carrie nodded. "Thank you." That was it. There was no other emotion on her face other than an impatient look. I stifled down my next words. It wasn't up to me to decide how someone grieved. I've read enough books to know everyone handles things in their own way and their own time.

I remembered a woman accused of murder who did cartwheels in the yard while the police were investigating. It didn't mean she was guilty. It just meant she was ... processing.

I could and did find it weird. I still couldn't decide she was a killer. That wasn't up to me.

"I'll go and get your book," I said, feeling awkward as I walked back to the office. I bent down at the safe and put in the combination. It opened and I pulled the book out, still in the bag I'd brought it in when I found Marcy. A shuddering sigh racked my body, and I stared blankly down at it for a moment. Life could end in a blink and all that was left were memories and things. I swallowed hard as I looked around my office. This was the culmination of a dream and a whole lot of money. If I had to leave it behind, the only one I had was my mother.

She liked to read, but she was retired. I didn't think she'd want to run this place.

I stood, my breath coming out slowly. Maybe after this I needed to make some changes. Make some friends. Get out in the world. Do more than read and work.

Marcy had wanted to, and she couldn't.

Shaken, I took the book back out and handed it to Carrie. "Here it is. If you want to come on over to the register, I'll ring you up."

Carrie opened the bag and pulled the book out. A

sneer lit her mouth briefly before she realized I was watching. "How much do I owe you?"

I rattled off the price as she pulled cash out of her wallet. "While I'm here, I'd also like you to find something else for me."

"No problem," I said politely. Harper hovered a few feet away, shifting nervously back and forth. "What book were you looking for?"

Carrie pulled a piece of paper out of her pocket. "A Law Dictionary by John Bouvier. I'm looking for the second volume, first edition."

I blinked at her and my eyebrows slowly rose. "Uh. Okay." That book was probably ten grand. "I know for a fact I don't have that one in stock. We don't stock anything over a few hundred dollars. Something like that will need to be paid for up front, including my five percent finder's fee. As long as you're okay with that, we can start the process."

Carrie nodded, her short dark hair swinging against her face. "That's fine."

I glanced over at Harper. She had a funny look on her face. A quick shrug lifted one of her thin shoulders and she turned away, pretending to straighten some files.

I gave Carrie her change back and pulled up my computer to try to find the book she was looking for. "Do you have all the other volumes?" I asked, trying to make conversation.

"My sister does." Our gazes met. Her dark one was curious, as I'm sure mine was. Maybe I was going about this all wrong. Maybe Carrie was just an introverted woman who collected rare books and had absolutely nothing to do with her sister's death. Maybe I was looking for something that wasn't there. She might be taller than her sister, but she still wasn't tall. In fact, she was a few inches shorter than me. I couldn't see her harming her sister and there was no evidence of a struggle in Marcy's house.

"Ah," I said as I found the book she was looking for. "If you'd like to look at this one, I think this might fit what you're looking for." I turned the screen around and let Carrie click on the pictures. Excusing myself, I walked over to where Harper was.

"This is so weird," she whispered, her voice barely audible. "Why is she worried about a book when her sister isn't even buried yet?"

"I don't know," I said, looking at Carrie. "But I hope to find out."

Carrie turned the monitor back around and nodded. "I'll take it," she said.

I came back over to the counter and rang up the purchase, adding in my fee. I didn't like Carrie that much, but I loved the $500 bucks I was making on this sale. She paid with a credit card and I swallowed hard as I swiped it. This was the single largest purchase I'd ever done, and I wasn't quite sure what to make of it. Usually people came in here asking for collectible books from their childhood. They weren't looking for books like these. Rarities like this wcrc for the big-time collectors. Not people like me or Harper.

"I should have it in within two weeks," I told her, pushing her purchase back over to her. "Enjoy your book."

Carrie nodded. Just as she started to walk away, Poppy came from behind a shelf and stopped in her path. The two females, feline and human, stared at each other. A heart wrenching yowl came from the red Persian. I gasped in alarm, but Poppy seemed fine. Just strangely ... vocal. She stared at Carrie as the woman stepped around her and walked away without another word, the jingling bell over the door the only sign she'd been here.

"Well, that is going to haunt me for the rest of the night," Harper said, her voice shaking.

"Me too." I went over to the cat and bent down to scratch her behind the ear. "You okay?"

Poppy meowed and promptly flopped on her back for a belly rub. I obliged, concern still making my thoughts spin. I'd never heard that sound come out of her before. "You don't like Carrie, do you?"

Poppy stared at me, her golden eyes betraying nothing of her thoughts.

"Neither do I," I murmured.

"Me too!" Harper chimed in. "That woman gives me the creeps."

The bell jingled again, and I sent Harper a warning look to stop talking about it. Greeting the woman who came in, I got up from the floor.

The customer smiled politely and went straight to the

romance section. Harper wiggled her eyebrows at me. "She has the right idea," she whispered.

"Shut it, Harper," I said.

My assistant and friend snorted in amusement and stretched.

Today could be a very long day.

BY THE TIME six rolled around, I was dead on my feet. An unexpected field trip rolled through and our shop was overrun with twenty exuberant fifth graders. When I saw them coming down the sidewalk, I had to stop myself from locking the doors. The money had the potential to be good and I couldn't begrudge kids a good book. I just didn't want them destroying my shop.

Two harried teachers came in and apologized profusely. One of them, a pretty strawberry blonde, spoke. "I am *so* sorry. We were supposed to go to a small farm two towns over, and when we got there, they had the place shut down! They didn't tell us or anything, and then we had twenty disappointed elementary school students! So, we had to call all their parents and the school and work something else out, and I am so sorry, but our kids will be careful. If they aren't, we will pay for everything. And if you have a cup of coffee, we will keep you in our prayers for the rest of our natural lives."

Harper burst out laughing. I motioned for them to come in. "We have a coffee pot over in the corner. It's your lucky day. We just made a fresh pot."

She sighed and eyed me like I was the best thing since sliced bread. Holding one finger up, she stepped back outside. I heard her barking orders to the kids like a drill sergeant and the kids began to file in, one at a time, whisper quiet.

I have no idea what she said to them, but it seemed to work.

Once we got them out the door and made a healthy profit from all the books they bought, I leaned against the counter and stretched out my aching back.

We hadn't been that busy in ages. "I think I need a chiropractor visit," I groaned.

Harper chuckled. "Those kids were adorable, weren't they?" I didn't miss the wistful note in her voice.

"They were," I agreed. "I can't believe how good they were."

"They were probably just delighted to be out of the classroom for the day. Kids need to get out more instead of sitting in the classroom all day." Harper shuffled some papers out of the way and began to wipe down the counter and the register. Exchanging cash all day and hosting customers paved the way for a lot of germs to get left behind so we wiped most surfaces down every day.

A quick glance at the clock made me stand up straighter. Five minutes until closing time! I took the other spray bottle and sprayed down the front of the desk, then walked over and cleaned off the door handles and the windows. By that time, the clock had struck six, and we were officially closed for business. On Fridays, we stayed open later and sometimes hosted a teen night, but the other days of the week we closed early. So far it hadn't hurt our bottom line and since we were in the area where a lot of tourists walked through, the hours made sense. By then a lot of them were out eating dinner or tired from the day and ready to go back to their lodging.

Waving at Harper, I grabbed my stuff and headed out the door. I wanted to stop by the investment firm who bought up all the properties on Marcy's street. All I had to do was a quick, anonymous public records search to figure out the investment firm's name and address.

TAPPING my nails on the austere white countertop, I waited for someone at the firm to notice I was alive. Granted, I guess I didn't look like I had a lot of free cash in my outfit of skinny jeans, rain boots and a long flannel. You shouldn't judge a book by its cover, even if it was true.

A woman with perfect makeup and what had to be a designer suit finally came over to me, her heels clicking across the floor in perfect timing to the music pumping through the speakers.

"Hello," she said politely. A quizzical look formed in her eyes. "Are you looking for someone?"

I smiled and put on my best *I am smart and I have every right to be here* look. Even though I didn't. I was about to get real nosy.

"Yes, hello. I'm interested in purchasing a house on Spruce Street, but when I went to my realtor's office, she told me that most of them were snatched up by an investment company." I smiled. "I'm here to figure out if there are any extra houses there for sale or if I could purchase one of them from you." I studied my nails. "You see, my boyfriend is an artist and when he came up to visit, he said one of those homes would be perfect for inspiration." I rolled my eyes. "But we didn't move fast enough when the one on the end came up for sale and now I'm here. I so want to be able to get him one for his birthday. You see, my parents left me a whole bunch of money, and I want to do something really nice for him."

It sounded lame even to my ears, but the woman's eyes widened when I mentioned the inheritance. Money. It always spoke. "Let me talk to my supervisors and see what they say," she said. She held up her index finger and walked away.

I watched her sashay for a minute, wondering how she kept her balance so perfect in those heels, before I wandered over to the seating area and settled in. This felt like buying a new car. If it went according to the way it usually did, the man behind the curtain would never come out, and I'd be left to deal with the woman at least twice until we settled on a price we could live with.

The other alternative was getting kicked out of here. I waited around to see which one it was going to be.

The office was impersonal in the way finance companies and banks usually were. The furniture was placed in perfect squares and made of metal and glass. Everything was chrome and black, the carpet a sedate gray. The walls were painted a neutral color, a shade somewhere between beige and gray. There was nothing about the place that suggested anyone human worked here. Not even a funny take a number sign.

The chair I sat on was uncomfortable, designed to get you in and out in minimum time, not the kind of place to get comfortable in.

The woman came back in less than two minutes, her smile a little stiff. "I'm sorry, what did you say your name was?" she asked.

I stilled. "I didn't." Studying her, I could see option number two, getting kicked out, was more likely now. "My name is Laura," I said. "Laura Kerringham." The lie rolled off my tongue easy enough to disturb me at the ease in which it came.

"Miss ... Kerringham," the woman began, "we can't divulge any information about those properties, nor can we sell you one."

"What about that one where the woman lives? I knocked on her door about a week before I came here. She was still living there, but I drove past today, and the house looks empty. Is that one for sale?"

She looked a little green around the gills. The door behind me opened, but I ignored it. "If you haven't bought that one, maybe I can get my realtor to check into it. I just assumed you guys had gone in and snapped that one up, too."

A man came out of an office just then. He was overweight with a receding hairline. His eyes flashed with anger as he walked toward me. I stood up, clutching my purse close to my body.

"Miss ... what did you say your name was?" He looked me up and down and finding me lacking, his posture relaxed as if he thought I wasn't a threat.

"Laura," I said.

"Laura," the man began, "what's your interest in the houses on Spruce? We couldn't sell any to you even if we wanted to. That land is scheduled to be developed soon." His eyes were shifty and there was a bead of sweat beginning to form on his forehead. I glanced down. The name Harvey was embroidered on his button-down shirt.

"But what about the house that hasn't sold?" I was so close to getting something. I knew it. Harvey was beginning to sweat just being around me and wasn't that curious?

"We are in negotiations with the owner of that home and will soon be in closing negotiations. I'm sorry we don't have better news for you." Anger made his eyes almost glow, and I took a nervous step back. There was something off about this Harvey character.

The sound of a throat clearing behind me made me spin around. I froze as soon as my gaze landed on a pair of familiar blue eyes and a stubborn jaw.

Hardy. Detective Cavanaugh.

Uh oh.

"Laura," Hardy said, his teeth clenching after he said my name, "may I speak with you a moment?"

I turned back to the investors. "So sorry. Thank you for your time."

I tried to breeze past Hardy, but he caught my arm and escorted me firmly outside.

The cold wind hit me right in the face and stole my breath, but Hardy didn't care. "What on earth are you doing?"

"Trying to get info!" I said, hearing the belligerence in my voice. "I want to know what happened to Marcy and I don't think you're doing a very good job at it."

Detective Cavanaugh's eyebrows rose. "Oh really? And what makes you, a bookseller, think you can do this better than us. Books? Is that it?" He exhaled a sharp breath. "There are a lot of rules to what we do, Laura, and if we don't do it right, we risk the offender getting off scot free. Your going in there and demanding info has the potential to damage our case!"

We stood, me looking up at him and him looking down at me. It was more glaring than looking and we stood that way for a least ten seconds before I blinked. Perhaps it was brash of me to do that. "I only wanted to help," I said.

"Maybe ask next time before you get some fool notion in your head like that."

I bristled. "I did get information, though," I said smugly.

"By pretending to be someone else," Hardy said. He shook his head. "We already knew about Carrie," he admitted. "With the new information we have, we are opening up a murder investigation." He pointed a finger at me. "One you need to stay out of. Are we clear?" His eyes were brilliantly blue, but this time I could see the fine lines fanning out from the sides of his face. This case was a strain on him. Silverwood Hollow was never a place where bad things happen so there must be a lot of pressure on him to solve this. Guilt flooded me, but I wasn't exactly sorry for what I'd done.

"Crystal," I muttered. So, it *was* a murder investigation. I tried not to puff up with pride. I knew Marcy hadn't died of natural causes. I would do my best to keep from trampling over Hardy's investigation, but I wouldn't be able to keep myself out of it anymore. "Have a good day, Detective."

He released my arm and gave me a long look. "Stay out of our way, Dakota. Every time you get involved, it has the potential to damage our case. I can only assume you don't want a murderer getting off because of your curiosity."

I huffed an annoyed breath and walked back to my car. I'd found out something major and Hardy knew it. Without waving goodbye, I started up my car and began to drive away.

I'd found out two things, actually. One, Carrie was already trying to sell the house and two, her case had been upgraded to murder. Something involving either those books or that land killed her.

I intended to find out which one it was. With or without Detective Cavanaugh.

ELEVEN

I unlocked the doors to Tattered Pages only to rush in and grab the ledger I'd been documenting for years. It was the same one the prior owner used. He'd delighted in showing me the thing, but when he opened up the closet in the back of the office and showed me fifty more of them, I'd been both impressed and horrified. He kept records of every single individual who'd come into the shop to order something.

Once I bought the place, I decided to keep those ledgers. Today I'd never been more glad of a decision. I flipped on one light and rushed to the back, fumbling with my cell phone to get the flashlight to turn on. I didn't want anyone banging on the door to be let in if they saw all the lights come on.

Within a minute I had the ledgers for the last five years and I was on my way out the door when I thought of something.

"Poppy!" I called. Sometimes the cat didn't want to come with me, and I left her in the shop. Those days were long gone, though. Once she realized I came with food and belly rubs, nine times out of ten she had no problem hitching a ride home with me. The one and only time I'd tried to leave her at my apartment, I'd come home to all of my new magazines shredded and her sitting in the middle of them like the queen of Sheba.

I did a quick search through the store, calling her name. When she didn't come, I figured she must have gone home with Harper. Poppy wouldn't leave during the middle of the day. It was like she knew this was her turf and she had to defend it.

I fired off a quick text to Harper. Before I'd finished locking the doors to the store, I had a picture of Poppy snuggling with Harper's adorable Calico. I grinned and shoved my cell back in my purse before I finished locking up.

Blowing out a frigid breath, I ran over to my car and got in, blowing on my hands as soon as I set the ledgers down in the passenger seat. It was positively frigid today. As soon as I started the car, I cranked the heat up to high and got on the road.

STEAM from the cup of tea I'd just made curled up and dissipated. I was more of a coffee drinker than a tea drinker, but it was cold outside, and I had way more coffee than I should have today. The first of the ledgers sat in front of me and I pored through the names, looking for any purchases made by Marcy or Carrie. I wasn't sure why I was looking, but I was curious to see if they'd made a habit of buying books even from the prior owner. I remember Marcy saying she'd been too sick to come out, but it didn't mean Carrie had never been by. I Googled their address to get their last name - Olds. I didn't know if I'd find something, but I checked both the first and last names on the off chance something came up.

I snorted to myself as I realized how much easier this would be if I had it on an Excel spreadsheet. The irony of it was not lost on me. I'm not sure why I kept documenting by hand, but there was something so comforting and nostalgic about it that I couldn't bring myself to put it on a file.

Maybe having to go through hundreds of names tonight would break me of that habit.

I'd owned the store for two years and during that time, I hadn't sold a lot of rare books. I didn't remember ever meeting the sisters before, but I still wanted to go through everything, just in case. I met a lot of tourists, so I wasn't sure how great my memory was after a couple of years.

I sipped my tea and slowly ran my finger down the book, pausing only when something similar popped up and I confirmed it wasn't them.

I got through my two ledgers quickly. When I picked up the third one and opened the page, I cringed. This wasn't just rare book documentation. The former owner documented every time he ordered a book, whether it was current or not. I sighed and went back up to fill my mug. On the way back to the table, I snagged a pack of cookies from the pantry. I'd have to be careful not to smear chocolate on the ledger, but I needed something to mindlessly snack on.

TWO HOURS LATER, I thought I might have something. A name had popped up a couple of times.

Martin Olds.

It was a strange enough name not to be common. I dialed up Mom.

"Hi honey!" she answered, her voice cheerful for almost ten o'clock at night.

"Hey Mom. Listen, have you ever heard the name Martin Olds?"

There was a pause. "Yes," Mom said, her voice now cautious. "Why?"

"I'm going through the old ledgers from the store and it looks like Martin came in several times a few years ago to order books."

"Oh, that's not surprising. That's Marcy and Carrie's father. He was an English Lit professor."

I remember Mom mentioning that. "It doesn't explain the books he was ordering, though. He bought some high value stuff."

"Hmm," Mom said. "Let me call Irma real quick. She'd know more than me. Can I call you back?"

"Sure. Thanks Mom." I hung up and jotted a note

down on the pad right beside me. Martin Olds had ordered a copy of the Gutenberg Bible which cost him over four grand. But the one that gave me great pause was an order for first edition UK paperbacks of the entire Harry Potter series. It had set him back almost thirty grand.

Was Marcy rich and just hadn't told anyone? Was that the reason she'd continually turned the investment group down?

I sat back in my chair, deep in thought. Was there an original set of Harry Potter books somewhere in Marcy's house?

My cell phone rang, startling me. I snatched it up. "Mom?"

"You aren't going to believe this," Mom said.

I curled my other hand around my mug. My heart began to pound. "What is it?"

"Martin was the heir to a fortune. I guess it's an open secret around here. Weird. I'd never heard it, but Irma knew about it. She knew his wife, though. I guess his parents patented some product back in the 50's and he was their only child."

My eyes widened in shock. "So, Marcy was rich," I breathed.

"Not necessarily," Mom cautioned. "She might have had a stipend or something set up in trust. I'm not really sure how it worked. All I know was Martin was well-liked, lived simply, and had a penchant for buying rare books and could afford to thanks to his parent's invention." Mom cleared her throat. "There's something else."

I wasn't sure I could handle it. "What is it?"

"There were some rumors that Carrie was adopted. Never substantiated," Mom cautioned. "I don't think the girls knew. But Martin was adamant that she was his. Neither of them ever wanted for anything."

"Whoa," I said. "Mom, this entire thing is so messed up. The police have upgraded this to a murder case. Someone took Marcy out. I just need to figure out why."

"Honey, you don't need to figure out anything. You need to step away and let the police do their job." Her voice, normally warm was urgent. "Whoever did this won't take kindly to you getting in the middle."

Hardy's words came back to me, warning me to stay away, but I felt like I could really help with this. "I don't feel like they're moving fast enough."

I could almost hear Mom shaking her head at me. "It isn't up to you. Stay out of this, Dakota. You aren't an investigator. You're a bookseller. It isn't your place."

"Love you," I said. "I gotta go."

"Dakota -"

I disconnected the call, wincing as I realized I just hung up on my mother. She was *definitely* not going to let me forget that one.

TWELVE

I was in dire need of a cupcake so about one minute before Trudy opened up shop, I was standing on her doorstep looking in the window making puppy dog eyes.

She rolled her eyes when she saw me standing there and rushed over to open the door. "Let me guess. It's been three days since you've had a cupcake and you're in sugar withdrawal?" Trudy grinned and held it open for me to come inside.

The warmth of the place made me sigh. Sometimes during the summer, it could get a little warm in here from all the ovens she used, but during the winter and fall, this place felt like I was sitting right in front of a toasty fireplace.

"It's pretty early in the morning," Trudy said as she let the door fall closed. "Are you wanting a muffin or a cupcake?"

I pulled my gloves off and walked over to the case she

was still setting up. There were pumpkin scones still available, but I always thought they resembled biscuits too much. I was more of a cake and muffin girl. "Do you have any chocolate chip muffins?" I looked back to see her re-tying her apron.

"Coming out of the oven in five minutes," she confirmed. "You want first dibs?"

I gaped at her. "A hot muffin fresh out of the oven with melty, delicious chocolate?" I'd died and gone to heaven. "Uh, yes please and thank you!"

Trudy snorted. "Have a seat. Grab a cup of coffee if you want and I'll get them out for you."

I clapped my hands together and impulsively reached over to hug her. "You're the best." I pulled my jacket off and slung it on the back of a chair. I looked around to make sure no one else had snuck in before I leaned in. "I just wanted you to know I got an early release of that book you've been waiting for. Technically, I'm not allowed to shelve it before next week but ..."

Trudy gasped and clapped her hands over her mouth. "Oh. My. God." Her eyes started to water, earning a laugh from me.

"The one with the wolves? And Chet Carter?" she whispered.

I nodded. "Uh huh. Pop over to the shop after work and Harper will let you in. I can't give it to you during business hours, but I'd be happy to smuggle it to you after hours."

"You are getting two muffins," Trudy said. "And two more tomorrow if you want them."

"My hips say yes, my scale says please for the love of everything, no." I laughed. "It's no problem, really. You're constantly feeding me, and I knew how much you wanted this book so ... It was the least I could do."

Trudy did a little dance on her way back to the kitchen. "I cannot wait!" she said as she disappeared into the back.

I wasn't a big romance reader, though I did love books with romantic subplots, so I couldn't get quite as excited as she was over the book. The author exploded onto the scene about a year ago with a complex tale of werewolves and their human mates. Trudy came into the store one day asking for them and I had to order the set from my supplier because I had no idea what she was talking about. Within three days, I had to order them again because I'd sold them all.

Werewolves and the women who loved them were big in this town. Who would have thought?

Trudy came out a few minutes later with two enormous muffins on a small plate. She'd stacked butter and a small knife on the side of it and when she placed it in front of me, the smell of chocolate wafted up.

"These look sinfully delicious," I said. I carefully cut into one and used my fork to take the first bite. They were so hot I would have burned my hand if I picked it up and tried to eat it that way.

Chocolate and sugar burst in my mouth. "Mmm," I said

and shut my eyes in bliss. "Trudy, you're a baking wizard. This was exactly what I needed."

"My pleasure. I tweaked the original recipe to make it more moist. Muffins aren't my specialty, but I thought these were good enough to sell."

I nodded enthusiastically; my mouth full with another bite. Trudy patted me on the shoulder and walked back behind the counter. "Take your time!" she called. "I have a little bit more to do before I'm a hundred percent ready for the day, but I'll be over to your shop right after six!"

I waved and focused all my attention on the muffin in front of me. I was going to be so full Trudy would have to roll me out of here, but this was the best muffin I'd ever fed my face with and I wasn't about to let any of it go to waste.

I WAS JUST PACKING up the second muffin when two women walked into the shop. They looked vaguely familiar, maybe people who'd wandered into the shop a few times. One of them was tall and thin, dressed in workout clothes and wearing a high ponytail in her dark blonde hair. The other was much shorter, her short dark hair clipped in a cute pixie cut. She was also dressed in workout clothes. If I had to exercise, you could bet the first thing I'd do when I got done was get a cupcake.

They stood in front of the case examining all the goodies when the blonde spoke. "Did you see the news this morning?"

The dark-haired one shook her head. "No, Charlie was

up until four this morning, so I didn't get up until close to 9." She yawned and stretched; her muscular arms taut.

"They said foul play was suspected in that woman's murder."

My fork stilled. I leaned a little further in to hear everything being said. I hadn't looked at the newspaper this morning and I was cursing myself.

"Foul play?" the dark one side, her voice disbelieving. "I wonder how they know that?"

The blonde lowered her voices. "I heard a rumor those sisters were heiresses, and they'd been fighting over that money for years."

"Really?" The brunette's brow furrowed. "Marcy and Carrie? My parents knew their mom and dad and they never mentioned anything like that."

The blonde nodded. "My boyfriend works at their attorney's office. He said Carrie is due in tomorrow to go over the will."

My eyebrows rose. First of all, her boyfriend should know better than to tell anyone that. I stood up, carefully setting the butter knife on the side of the plate. "Excuse me," I said.

"Yes?" the blonde said, her tone cool as she looked me up and down, casting aspersions on my outfit I could only guess.

"I'm interested in that case," I said. "I couldn't believe when I read it in the paper. Such a shame. She was a nice woman. I never knew she was an heiress."

"Yeah," the blonde snorted. "That's because she never

spent any money. Apparently, the younger sister, Carrie, was the one with a penchant for spending. My boyfriend says she got a tiny allowance compared to what her sister did." She shrugged one perfect shoulder. "I'd be mad about it, too. I bet she offed her."

I blinked. "Excuse me?"

The woman rolled her eyes. "I mean, you don't think her sister killed her to get her hands on that cash?" She made an unflattering scoffing sound. "I heard that house was full of valuable things. And now she gets to keep them all."

The brunette frowned at her friend. I wonder if she knew how bloodthirsty she was before this happened.

"Well, I don't know what happened. It's a tragedy all the way around," I said.

The blonde snorted. "It ain't a tragedy for whoever's getting all that cash." She turned around when Trudy cleared her throat.

Trudy's eyes met mine in warning. Right. Don't antagonize the customers. I walked back over to the table and grabbed my stuff. Right before I walked out the door, I raised my hand in farewell.

Trudy returned the gesture before she turned her attention back to the two women.

The will reading was soon. I wonder if Hardy knew about it. Just as I was about to reach for the door, it opened and in walked the man himself.

I touched my throat in surprise. "Oh, hi!"

The detective nodded to me once, his blue eyes flashing. So, he was still annoyed with me about yesterday. I huffed and was about to walk past him when he leaned down. "Remember what I said." Hardy's gaze pinned me. A thunderous frown formed on my face and I was about to give him a piece of my mind when he stepped away and let the door go.

I fumbled with my jacket and bag to catch it. "Jerk," I muttered before I stepped into the cool Virginia air.

HARPER WAS on the phone motioning wildly with her hands when I walked back into the store.

"Oh, yes! Dakota is here! Hold on," she said and waved the phone receiver at me.

My shoulders slumped. It was probably something about the Harvest Fest coming up. I took the phone and a woman's voice immediately came over the line.

"Dakota Adair, this is Corky." I knew who it was. Few people had that gravelly voice or steel in their spine.

"Hello, Auntie," I said, grinning because I knew she hated that name.

"I'm calling because I heard you were planning the festival again this year." She ignored my use of Auntie, so she needed something. Otherwise I wouldn't have gotten away with it.

"I am," I said, not offering any other information.

"I'd like to be a judge in one of the contests."

I pressed my lips together to keep from laughing. "Which one?" I knew which one, the sly little devil.

"'The drink category."

"Aunt Corky, you do know we haven't decided if we were going to allow alcohol yet, right?"

Her sigh of annoyance was epic. "What kind of contest is it for adults if you don't allow a little libation?" she demanded. "Really, Dakota. I think I'm going to have to speak to your mother about this."

"I'm thirty-three," I reminded her gently. "I think I'm old enough to decide something like this."

"Regardless," she huffed. "I'd like to judge."

"Even without booze?" I asked, surprised.

"Dakota, I'm embarrassed for you. You act like I'm some kind of a boozehound!" She actually sounded offended. I rolled my eyes. This was the woman who strapped on a flask and wore it like a fashion accessory.

"I would never, Auntie," I said.

She scoffed. "Yes or no, honey. I don't have all day."

A laugh escaped me. "Fine, Corky. You can judge. But if you do anything embarrassing, I'm going to ban you from the festival next year."

A cackling laugh came over the line. "Now why would I do that? I'd never embarrass my favorite niece, would I?"

"Don't test me, Corky!" I warned.

She made a kissy noise over the line. "Ta, darling. I'll see you in a few weeks."

I disconnected the line and looked over to Harper who was trying not to laugh. "Don't even," I said. "She's a handful."

"I love Aunt Corky," Harper said. "I hope I'm like her when I get old."

"Boozy and annoying?" I asked.

Harper snorted. "Out there and carefree," she corrected.

"It seems like too much work," I grumped. I shed my jacket and scarf and vowed to buy a heavier sweater when I needed to step outside for just a minute.

The bell over the door jingled only to reveal Cole standing there, his hair adorably windblown and the tip of his nose red. I sighed in annoyance. He was cute, but I didn't want him in my store.

"Go away, Cole," I said before I started to walk to the office.

Harper gasped. "Dakota!"

Cole held up a hand. "It's okay. I deserved it." He jogged over to me. "I need to talk to you."

"About what?" I demanded, tilting my face to look up at him. It annoyed me that I had to. His gaze danced with amusement.

He looked around the shop and dipped his head next to my ear. "The Olds. It's important."

I chewed on my lip as I studied him. "Fine," I said after a moment. "Come to the back."

Cole followed behind me and slipped inside the office. I shut the door and gestured for him to sit. His lanky frame sank into the extra chair and I sat in the rolling one. "I have no idea why you're here or why you think I'm interested in this," I said.

"Please. I know you've been looking into Marcy's death. Let's not kid each other."

My eyes narrowed. "And how would you know that?"

His eyebrows wiggled and a grin slowly slid onto his adorably handsome face.

"You - you were following me?" I asked, outrage filling me.

"Of course, I was," he said, stretching his hands out in a gesture for peace. "I'm a journalist."

"You're such a jerk!" I screeched. I was about to stand up, when he held his hand up.

"Please. I'm serious. Just wait. I found out something you'll be interested to hear."

Curiosity won out over my anger. "Then tell me."

"Carrie is the sole heir. There's no one left in the family. She gets everything." Cole adjusted his glasses. "But that's not all. I caught her meeting with the guy in charge of that investment firm. From - ah - what I saw it was more than a professional meeting."

My eyebrows rose. "The bald guy? Harvey something or other? They're dating?"

Cole chuckled, an embarrassed flush rising on his skin. "I'd say they're doing more than that."

A surprised laugh rang from me and I clapped a hand over my mouth. "Oh my. That can't be professional." I remembered the way he looked at me and a chill ran down my spine. Harvey did not like me there asking questions about those properties.

"No. I'm not sure what's going on there, but I'm not a hundred percent sure Carrie is the guilty party here."

"What?" I asked, staring at him like he'd grown a second head. "Why not? Sole heir and hamming it up with the company who wanted to buy Marcy out?"

He shook his head. "I'm not sure. Just a feeling."

Cole was a journalist. Those feelings probably paid off for him quite often. I crossed my arms over my chest. "I still think Carrie is involved somehow. In fact, she should be the only suspect." My brow furrowed as I thought about it. "Unless you think the guy could be in on it, too." I gasped. "Or maybe he guilted her into it?"

Cole sighed. Crossing one ankle over his knee, he leaned forward a little. "We're missing something here," he said. "Do you know how she died?"

I shook my head. "They won't release that information."

A frown lit his mouth. "Yeah, they didn't have it in the story either. They're being tight lipped about it. I wonder why."

I thought about finding Marcy. "I couldn't see anything wrong with her when I found her."

Cole's brow wrinkled. "No blood? Nothing?"

I shook my head. "She was a little blue around the mouth, but that's all. There was a weird smell in the house, though. I couldn't place it."

"Weird how?" Cole's expression was eager, and I remembered who I was talking to.

A breath escaped me. "That's all I'm going to tell you."

"Come on! I just gave you some juicy details." Hurt flashed in his eyes, but I held firm. He was still a journalist.

"Also, stop following me." I stood up and opened the door for him to leave.

"I can't promise anything," he said as he stood up and walked over to me. Just as he was about to exit, he leaned over close to my ear. "Interesting things seem to happen around you, Dakota Adair." He winked and walked away.

I sank against the door frame and tried not to watch him walk away.

It was a losing battle.

As soon as the door closed, Harper swooned. "He is so cute!" she stage whispered. "How in the world have you not asked him out?"

I waved a tired hand at her. "Not interested. He's way too nosy for his own good."

"So what?" Harper said. "That's his job. He's the cutest thing to arrive in this town for years!"

"Then you go ask him out," I said. I turned back around and shut myself in my office for a little while.

This thing with Marcy was wearing me out.

THIRTEEN

Jeff caught me just as I was about to get into my car.

"Dakota!" he called.

I stopped, my hand on the door and turned. Jeff ran toward me, his tie swinging with the motion.

"I'm so glad I caught you!" he said.

I was so not in the mood to deal with him today. "If this is about my business, I don't want to hear it, Jeff. I've had a weird day."

He chuckled and shook his head. "Not today. I promise." He looked around the street to make sure we were alone. "Listen, I have it on good authority that paperwork was done to purchase Marcy's house before she passed away. Without her authorization."

I straightened, my hand slipping from the door. "By whom?"

Jeff swallowed hard, his eyes looking at everything. "The investment company. The only way that could have happened is if Marcy signed over Power of Attorney to Carrie."

I sank against my car. "And then she wound up dead, allowing the sale to go through a lot quicker." Maybe Carrie hadn't done it. Why would she have killed her sister when she was getting what she wanted anyway?

Jeff nodded. "I don't know what's happening with this, but there's something really off with the timing."

"You're right." Why in the world was he helping me? "Are you looking for Harper?"

His jaw clenched. "I'm not an idiot, Dakota. I know you don't like me and I'm not here just to get in good with Harper." He rubbed the back of his neck. "Although a nice word from you would probably go a long way."

I shook my head and was about to climb into my car when he spoke again. "Look. I don't like this business any more than you do. The last thing I want people to think is I harm people when they don't give me what I want. This is business. I don't want any bad juju rubbing off on me." A rueful smile crossed his face, quick as lightning. "It doesn't mean I'm going to stop badgering you to sell your shop, though. You have prime time real estate here."

"Goodbye, Jeff," I said as I climbed into my car.

His face fell. Sympathy flooded me and right before I closed the door I said, "I might put in a good word for you."

Jeff looked like Christmas came early.

"Maybe," I said right before the door slammed.

It didn't deter him. A wide grin split his face as he

turned to walk away. He shoved his hands in his pockets, but his step was a little lighter than it had been before.

What in the world was happening in this town? Jeff being a decent human being? It felt like the world had turned upside down.

On my way home, thoughts of the Power of Attorney stuck in my mind. The will reading was tomorrow. Maybe I could slide in there and pretend I was a long lost relative?

No. That's crazy. Carrie would recognize me in a heartbeat. How could I get ears in there? My heart beat faster as I remembered the one person I could always call when I wanted to do something a little offbeat.

Grandma.

Granted, this was less offbeat and more illegal, but Gran always shot me straight and gave me advice when I was considering doing something to get myself in trouble. I was a good girl growing up and in college, too, but I was mischievous. More than the average bear.

I voice called Gran because Virginia was a hands-free cell phone state, something I forgot periodically but was trying to be good about.

She answered on the second ring.

"Hello? Dakota, is that you?"

"Hey Gran," I said, my chest warming at her voice. She lived a couple towns over, and I didn't get to see her as much as I once did.

"You should come visit me more," she said, her voice kind but admonishing.

"I know. How about you come to the Harvest Festival

this year? I'll come over and pick you up. Aunt Corky is judging a portion of our fall drink contest."

"Oh, that's a terrible idea!" I knew she was talking about Corky and not coming to town. "She's going to be sloshed in the first twenty minutes!"

"She pulled the family card. I didn't really have a choice."

"Maybe you should add an extra judge in and then pull all of her scores out." Grandma laughed long and loud at that. It wasn't a terrible idea.

"I'll consider that," I said, chuckling about how confused Corky would be. "Listen, Gran, I have an issue I want to talk to you about."

There was a pause on the line. "Is it illegal?"

"Maybe?" I wasn't sure if it was or not. Posing as a relative sounded iffy at best, and illegal at worst.

"Let it rip," she said. I could hear yapping in the background. "Terminator, hush!"

I stifled a snort. My grandma had what was best called a menagerie of pets, all of them with super weird names. She had Terminator, the yappy Chihuahua. Rocky Balboa, the drooling bulldog. A cat named Fancy Feast, a bird named Twiggy, and a ferret named Mickey Mouse. I hadn't seen her in a few months, so the odds of her having a new animal were pretty high. Gran owned a couple of acres out there and it seemed like there was a network of stray animals out there who whispered Gran's name to each other if the going got tough.

"If I wanted to go to a will reading, but I wasn't a family member, how would I do that?"

Gran laughed. "I can only assume you aren't invited either?"

"Not even a little bit."

"Wellll," she drawled. "There's no such law that a will has to be read. Do you know for sure a reading is actually happening?"

"As far as I know." I still needed to find out where the reading was, but it couldn't be too hard. The towns surrounding this place weren't all that large and there weren't too many law firms out there.

"I'd recommend waiting for the will to be filed in the courts. Then it becomes public record. But if you want to know right away, I'd try to convince someone else to get in there for you."

"I don't have anyone who would do that for me," I said. Disappointment made my shoulders slump.

"I don't have anything going on this week," Gran said. "Retirement can get pretty boring sometimes."

I perked up. "You want to do this?"

"Of course, I do, Dakota girl! When's the last time we've gotten to do anything illegal together?"

Laughter burbled from me. "High school is the last time I can remember." Gran helped me break into a boy's car and fill it with marbles. He wouldn't stop harassing me and reporting it to the school did no good. When I told Gran what happened, she wanted to do worse - fill it with bubble bath and stick a hose through the sunroof to flood it out. When I mentioned we might have to pay for the value and possibly go to jail, she backtracked. Some. It still wasn't out of the realm of possibility for her. I convinced her to do something dry - something that would be a real pain to get out.

We settled on marbles and a creepy note that said, "Keep your hands to yourself." He had no idea who it came from because he put his hands on all kinds of girls. Pretty sad.

Gran and I hid in the bushes after he left a party one night. The look on his face I'd never forget. He was comically outraged and super creeped out when he got the note.

Two weeks later, he was back to groping girls, so Gran and I had to get a little more creative. She had me contact all the girls he'd been accused of messing with and we gathered them all in one room. Gran paid an actor to dress up as a police officer, and we lured the kid to the house under the guise of a candlelit dinner for two. The kid, Gary, thought he was going to score, but when one of the girls lured him into the living room, he got an intervention with twelve angry teenage girls and a man who was being paid very well to pretend if Gary didn't cut it out, he was going to be serving a long prison sentence with a lot of angry men who didn't like boys who abused girls.

Gary ended the night in sobbing tears and had to be driven home by the fake police officer. I was remorseful after it was over, but Gran was ecstatic. "I bet that teaches him. His parents should be ashamed of themselves!"

I thought for sure we were all going to jail, but we

scared Gary enough to where he never said a word about what happened, and neither did any of the other girls involved. Most of them moved away from this place, but every once in a while, I saw Lila and we shared a secretive smile.

Gary was a perfect gentleman after that and ended up marrying one of the girls from his senior class. He doesn't come into the store but occasionally I'd see his wife.

"I saw Gary the other day," Gran said. "That's a completely different young man than he used to be." She didn't say thanks to us, but I knew that's what she was thinking.

"I still can't believe we did that."

"It worked!" Gran said and that's all she needed to know. She didn't care about getting into trouble and it was even worse now that she was older. "Tell me where I need to be and what time I need to be there, and I'll make sure I'm there."

"Are you sure you want to do this?" Part of me felt guilty about sending an elderly woman into spy, but Gran ate stuff like this up.

"Of course, I do! People don't let old people participate in things anymore. It's maddening. I'm old, not dead or crippled."

"I'll pick you up and take you, just in case we need to beat a hasty exit, okay?"

"Alright, darling. You give me a call as soon as you have the details."

We disconnected just as I pulled into the driveway.

. . .

LESS THAN AN HOUR LATER, I knew exactly where the will reading was going to be. Houghton, Harper, and Hooker, not too far away from here in Silverwood. The place had all kinds of rumors about it, the last one about it being overran with cats. The rumors had been flying for a while about some of the lawyers in that practice, but I didn't see what the fuss was about. I considered most things to fall in either the none of my business or the I don't care category. Maybe the lawyers would let Gran in. They seemed kooky enough to go along with it. We didn't have a lot of law firms around here so the ones we did have had to be prepared to do all kinds of paperwork. You never knew what was going to happen in this town.

I called Gran back and gave her the details and then called Harper to tell her I'd be late. When she pushed me for details, I told her I was going to lunch with my grandma so she wouldn't push. She needed plausible deniability just in case this thing went south. I didn't think anyone would arrest an 80+ year old woman, but you never knew in this town.

I wanted to know exactly what was being said about this will and if Carrie had any other family coming out of the woodwork who might act as a beneficiary.

I stretched and grabbed myself a sandwich. I wanted to get to bed early tonight. Tomorrow promised to be a crazy day. Fingers crossed Grandma still had it in her to participate in shenanigans.

. . .

GRAN OPENED the door wearing a hideous pair of purple pants and an orange sweater. I blinked several times before I said good morning to her.

"Is there a reason you're wearing that?" I asked politely.

"Honey, you don't show up as an out of town, unknown relative wearing black. I need to be unknown for a reason!" she exclaimed. She reached down into a brown paper bag at her feet and pulled out a massive feather boa. "Is this too much?" she asked, flinging it around her neck dramatically.

"Umm. Yes. Way too much, Gran." I pressed my lips together to keep from laughing as she sashayed around the house, flicking the boa left and right.

"How do you do, dahling," she drawled to no one in a terrible French accent. "My name is Fifi LeFay and I am here to ensure you see nothing of your inheritance. I am zee lost love child of your father and the famous French movie star, Cameron LeRoux."

My shoulders shook with laughter as I watched her, even as I hoped she didn't really hope to gain access to the law firm acting like that.

She was in her eighties but looked early sixties. Her figure was trim and compact, and she stood about two inches shorter than me. She kept her hair a sedate red, colored once a month at a salon down the road, and chin length so it swung dramatically as she spoke. Normally, she wore little makeup, just enough to give herself some pizzazz. But today, she'd taken it to an entirely new level.

She wore bright red lipstick and enough rouge on her face to make her look like she was late for circus practice. Her eyelashes were so long she looked like she was wearing two spiders on her eyelids. The only thing halfway sensible about her this morning was her shoes.

Gran loved her tennis shoes so much that if she had to wear a dress, she'd complain about the shoes all night and accuse them of being torture devices designed by the Nazi's to subjugate women.

She was delightfully weird and one of my favorite people. "I'm a little concerned about this," I warned. "You aren't going to pretend to be French, are you?"

She spun around, her sneakers squeaking on the tile floor. "Of course not. I'm just warming up to get into character. I'm going to be her father's birth mother, discovered only through new DNA evidence. You hear about all those DNA tests going up on that 23 site? Whatever it is? It's not unheard of for people to find new moms and dads and brothers and sisters. All those people should be ashamed of showing up to church on Sunday with all those sins riding around in their britches!"

It was out there, but it could work. It might shatter Carrie's illusion of her father, but she didn't seem like a super good person any way. It still bothered me. "Are you sure that's the best idea? What about maybe a cousin or something? Someone not directly linked to her father or mother? I just want to make sure she wasn't involved in her sister's death, not ruin her life."

"Psssh," she said. "You think this woman murdered her sister, don't you?"

"I'm not real sure, Gran. Maybe. I'm just gathering info now."

She stared hard at me, her brow furrowing. "Fine. I'll be a cousin then. A first cousin."

Gran was awfully old to be a first cousin. "Maybe just keep it vague, then."

"You're a lot less fun now that you're in your thirties," Gran grumbled.

"Come on, old lady," I said good naturedly. "Let's get you in the car so we can get into trouble."

Gran picked up the paper bag by the front door and walked out.

"What's in the bag?" I asked as I made sure the door locked behind me.

"Sunglasses, just in case I need them. A wig, in case I decide to be someone else. I got a notepad, thinking maybe I could be a reporter. And two bottles of those energy drinks, just in case I need to run out real quick like." Her eyes went shifty. "And a couple more things in case of an emergency."

This was a mistake. I could feel it in my bones. Opening the door for Gran, I helped her in the car. "This is going to be a disaster," I murmured more to myself than her.

"Sure is!" she agreed good naturedly. "Make sure you keep the car running just in case we need to make a quick getaway!"

It took less than ten minutes to get to the law firm. I made Gran keep all of her props in the bag, even the wig. She leaned over, patted me on the hand, and slid out of the car, spry for a woman her age. The prospect of mischief put a spring in her step, and I clasped my hands over my mouth to keep from cracking up as she pranced up the steps. My phone rang, and I opened it without looking.

"I'm going to keep the line open," Gran stage whispered. I looked over to see her speaking into her purse.

A snort of laughter escaped. "Good idea, Gran. Now get inside and get some info!"

My heart was beating double time as she opened the doors to the firm. A woman with a friendly voice greeted her. "Hello, my name is Sara. Can I help you?"

"Yes, you can," Gran said, thankfully without a French accent. "I'm here for the will reading of one Marcy Olds. Her father and my lover were best friends, and he promised us we'd be in the will!"

Hysterical laughter burst from me. My gran was certifiable.

You could hear a pin drop in the room.

"Um, excuse me," a male voice said. "Who are you again?"

"My name is Carmen!" Gran declared. "I demand to be let in!" There was a shuffle and the sound of a door slamming open came through the line.

"As you can see, Miss Olds, your father has left you everything, including the collection of rare -" The voice broke off. "Excuse me? You cannot be in here!"

"It's a free country," Gran shouted. "And you there, your father owes me a house in the country and an apple orchard!"

"Who *are* you?" Carrie's voice came, shocked and annoyed.

Static came over the line, then, and all I could hear was bits and pieces. "Get out, Gran," I murmured to myself. "Get out, get out, get out."

"Ma'am," the male voice said, the reception becoming clearer again, "I'm going to have to ask you to leave!"

"I want what's mine!" Gran said, her voice becoming a hysterical wail.

"You don't have anything in here that's yours!" Carrie shouted. "It's all mine! I finally get what should have been mine from the beginning!"

With that, stunned silence fell. My mouth fell open.

"Well," Gran said, "with that little nugget, I suppose I ought to be on my way."

"Oh my gosh," I whispered. I started the car and backed out of the spot. I pulled as close as I could to the door.

It sounded like Gran was running. As fast as an eighty-year-old could run anyway. I watched as the doors burst open and an orange and purple flash sped toward my car. I reached over, opened the door, and Gran slid in, a maniacal grin on her face. "Go go go!" she shouted and then began to laugh like a crazy person.

Hysterical laughter spilled from me as she slammed the door. I mashed the gas, and we sped out of the law office parking lot like bloodhounds were after us.

"Woo!" Grandma exclaimed. "Did you hear all that? Carrie! That woman is some piece of work. Wanting what her daddy had and not content with what he'd given her. She has to be guilty!"

Pride burst within me. "That was awesome, Gran. A little nuts, but you got what I needed." We were almost out of Glendale and going a more sedate speed, when a Toyota Avalon pulled up behind me.

Oh. No. My eyes widened as I looked in the rearview.

Detective Hardy Cavanaugh was behind me and he did *not* look amused.

FOURTEEN

Gran isn't concerned until Hardy turned on his lights to get me to pull over. "Oh my stars!" she exclaimed. "Are we getting pulled over?" Gran clapped her hands together. "Do you think we'll get arrested, Dakota?"

I debate mashing the gas pedal down and hauling butt out of there but then we really would get arrested. "Admit nothing, Gran." I eyed her purple and orange outfit. "Do you have anything else in that bag?"

Gran eyed me. "Like a change of clothes?"

Her eyes gleamed. "'Course I do. I wasn't sure what character I was going to play, so I brought a few things."

"How fast can you change?" I looked down at the speedometer. 55 miles per hour. I could pretend my brakes weren't working all that well and that's what took me so long to slow down.

"Honey, I still got mad flexibility," Gran answered. "I

take yoga down at the Y every few days. There's this cute instructor named Hans. He has buns of -"

"Gran!" I pinched my brow. "Grab something not so ... loud and change. Just make sure he can't see you." My gaze flicked to the rearview mirror.

Gran gives me a contemplative look. "Do you know that man?"

"I do and he is not going to be happy with me." I very gently started to decrease my speed.

Gran reached down and rummaged through the bag. She pulled out a pair of old sweatpants and a sweatshirt that said, "Granny Gangster." I don't even want to know where she got it from.

Gran hunched down in the seat and shrugged out of the orange monstrosity of a sweater. She shoved it back in the bag and pulls the sweatshirt over her head. She didn't bother slipping out of her pants. Gran just shoved her shoes off and pulled the sweatpants right over the purple ones.

"Thanks, Gran," I whisper. "Also, that sweatshirt is horrendous."

"I got it at a rap concert," she volunteered. "It was Senior Night at the Bingo Hall and also open mic. A couple of friends of mine fancy themselves rappers like that Nicki Minaj. They keep claiming their milkshake is bringing all the boys to their yard. I don't know what that means, but milkshakes give me the runs, so I don't drink them anymore."

I cringe and pray I never have to explain the meaning

of that song to my grandmother. Ever. "That's nice, Gran," I said, my voice faint.

"So, who's the young buck behind us and what does he want with you?" Gran is peering in the rearview. "He looks like he's cute. My vision isn't what it used to be, but that jawline looks like it could cut glass!"

I couldn't put it off any longer, so I slowly pulled off to the shoulder. I turned off the car, gave my grandma a look, and exhaled a deep breath. I was *so* not looking forward to this.

"Deny everything, Gran, okay? Everything."

"You got it, kiddo. They can't prove it was me." She cackled and put her hands in her lap like she was an innocent old lady. The sweatshirt screamed she was not, but maybe I could claim she was homeless, and I was only driving her to a restaurant for a meal.

They could most definitely prove it was her if they had surveillance. Hardy tapped on the window.

His amazing jawline was taut, and his eyes sparked with anger. I pressed the button to roll down the window.

He leaned in, resting his arms on the bottom of the window. "Hello, Dakota." His voice was calm and measured which told me one thing.

He was positively furious.

"Hello, Hardy," I said, my face frozen in a smile.

Gran leaned over. "I'm Dakota's grandma. She didn't tell me she knew such a fine, young specimen of man!"

Hardy blinked, his face a picture of confusion. I

pressed my lips together to keep from laughing. And crying. I wasn't sure what I wanted to do right now.

"Uh. Hello, ma'am."

Gran reached over and extended her hand. "Charlotte Adair," she said.

He took it. "Hardy Cavanaugh."

"Now that's a nice strong name. So many boys growing up given stupid names like Chet or Bowser or Richard." She sighed. "Hardy shows confidence and strength. Tell me, how do you know my granddaughter?"

Hardy was nonplussed. His chest rumbled a short laugh. "We met on an investigation."

"Oh, isn't that nice? And so romantic. Now answer me a question. Are you going to ask her out?"

"Gran," I hissed. "It isn't like that."

Gran reared back and examined me. "And why not? You're single. This young man isn't wearing a ring so I can only imagine he's single." She peered at him. "Are you single? Or do you have some girl pining away for you?"

"Ah, I'm single," he said. His gaze lingered on my burning face.

"Well then, you won't find another girl in the entire area of Silverwood Bay sweeter, prettier, or smarter than my granddaughter."

A grin was peeking out from the side of his mouth. "Maybe not. But that isn't why I stopped her, Mrs. Adair. I got a complaint of an elderly woman causing a ruckus at the local law firm." His eyes lit on my gran. "Do you happen to know anything about that?"

She batted her eyes up at him. "Do I look like I know anything about that or causing a ruckus? I'm 84 years old! The only kind of ruckus happening in my life is when I forget to go down to the knitting shop and buy the right kind of yarn for my project." She clutched her hip. "In fact, that's where we were going to now. You see my hip acts up - arthritis, so it's hard for me to drive some days."

"I see," Hardy said. A put-upon sigh escaped him. "Dakota, I hope you're heeding my warning to stay out of this case. It's awfully convenient that Ms. Olds had a will reading today and we get a report of two women hauling tail out of a parking lot in a car they described as almost identical to yours."

"I have an impeccable driving record," I said. "Not a single speeding ticket. I'm not the kind of person who "hauls tail" Detective. I own a bookstore for goodness' sake."

Hardy exhaled a breath, tapped once on my roof, and stood up. "Have a nice day, Ladies," he said before he began walking back to his car. Gran unbuckled her seat belt, leaned over me, and stared out my window at his retreating form.

"You could do a lot worse than him, Dakota," she said when she was finished ogling him.

"I don't even want to talk about it, Gran." I started the car up and drove away. "You were supposed to stay quiet."

"I threw him off balance, honey. You did notice he didn't ask a whole lot of questions, didn't you?"

I did. I glanced over at her.

"Men don't like to be put on the spot about asking

someone out for a date. He wanted to run away screaming."

A snort escaped me.

"So, you should thank me."

My lips quirked in a smile. "Thank you."

"And stop for ice cream up here to the right," Gran demanded. "I need something sweet to help balance out all that adrenaline."

FIFTEEN

Carrie Olds stood in my shop, holding up an old copy of Watership Down. Harper took it from her and gently laid it down on the counter.

"I was wondering if you could appraise this," she said. "It's one of the few my father didn't leave a value on." Carrie looked sallow and tired. An oversized cardigan hung on her shoulders. She wore no makeup and her lips were cracked and dry.

I sidled up to Harper and examined the book. It was a hardback and looked to be an original first edition. I bent down to grab a pair of cloth gloves from under the counter and slipped them on before I opened the book.

"Rex Collings," I murmured. My finger landed on the copyright date. "1972." I flipped a few more pages and realized the book was signed. My goodness. This family had some extremely valuable literary works in their possession. My nose tickled as a strange smell filtered up from the book. Something nudged at the back of my mind at the scent, but I couldn't place it.

I flipped through all the pages and noted the book was in really good condition. "With a cursory glance, I'd say this is probably worth at least four grand."

Carrie's eyes gleamed with avarice. "Really?" she asked and snatched it out of my hand before I could close the book.

"Really," I said shortly. "But it smells a little strange. Do you notice that?"

Carrie's face went blank. "I hadn't noticed," she said, her words short and clipped.

Poppy chose that moment to hop up on the counter next to me. She sat perfectly still, pinning Carrie with her intense golden eyes. I reached over to give her a scratch on the head, but Poppy didn't move an inch or even acknowledge my presence. All her attention was on the woman in front of me.

Carrie looked away first and cleared her throat, uncomfortable with the scrutiny she was under.

I slipped off the gloves and put them back where I found them. "Good luck with it," I said and left her standing there with Harper. That was probably rude, but I still wasn't convinced she was innocent. I headed back to the office where I had a salad waiting for me in the fridge. It was karma for all those cupcakes I'd been eating lately.

. . .

I'D JUST LOCKED the doors when a soft knock on the window alerted me to another visitor. Harper had already gone for the day. "We're closed!" I called, not bothering to look to see who it was.

The knock came again and when I peeked around, Cole's handsome face was at the window. He waved urgently. My shoulders slumped, but I went to unlock the door for him.

"Dakota!" he said. "I have some news." He didn't bother to unbutton his coat as he stepped inside.

"I don't want to hear it." I did, but I didn't want to hear it from Cole. He was fast becoming a pain in my backside.

"You're going to want to hear this." His face grim, he walked over and collapsed into one of the seats. "One of my sources was able to take a peek at Marcy's death certificate."

My brows rose high. I took the seat next to him.

"Interested now?" Cole chuckled and peeled his gloves off. "Formaldehyde poisoning."

I rocked back in my chair; brow furrowed. "Formaldehyde..." I murmured. My eyes widened, and I inhaled sharply. "That's what that smell was!" I slammed my palms down on the table. "I smelled it when I went into her house and when she brought a book over."

Cole leaned forward, his gaze sharp with concern. "Carrie was here?"

"A few hours ago." I waved off his concern. "There's formaldehyde present in the ink used on books. Could it be what was making Marcy sick?"

The journalist was staring at me, his mouth wide open. "Formaldehyde in printing ink?"

"Yes. It's present in a lot of household things." I thought back to the sheer amount of books in that house. "Cole, do you know any of the symptoms Marcy was experiencing before she died?"

He blinked and sat back. "Umm, some, I guess. Interviews with people who knew her said she was tired all the time. She had vision trouble and symptoms of a common cold. Low blood pressure." He shrugged. "I can't remember them all, but I have it back in the office."

I tapped my chin. "I wonder how long she'd had those books in her house."

"Her father passed away five years ago, I think. I can only assume around that long." Cole scrubbed a hand over his face before he sat straight up, his spine rigid. "Dakota." He turned wide eyes to me. "Carrie has a degree in chemistry. She was fired from a lab in Bangor for unauthorized experimentation."

A crash shattered our hushed words. Cole reached for me and pulled me against him, knocking over the chairs. I stumbled against him and landed in his lap.

Something thudded on the floor of the store. Cole stood, pulling me with him and looked down at the ground. A small metal canister rested on the floor.

"We have to get out," Cole said, urgency in his tone.

The canister started to tremble and hiss. White smoke poured out of it from both ends.

"Use your shirt to cover your nose!"

Terror rang through my bones. I pulled my shirt over my nose and mouth and let him lead me to the back. His steps were sure and fast. "Window?" he called as he turned back to look at me.

My eyes watered and tears ran down my face. I wordlessly pointed to the back.

Cole led me down the maze of shelving and to the back. With two solid kicks, he broke one of the windows. He took his jacket off, wrapped part of it around his hand and punched out the rest of the glass.

A horrible thought occurred to me. I pulled away from him and stumbled back into the main area of the shop. "Poppy!"

My gaze swung wildly as I tried to find the Persian. A loud cry to the left had me lurching forward. The cat sat there, eyes wide, and voice yowling. I scooped her up quickly and rushed back to the window. I gently pushed Poppy toward the window. Without a look back, Poppy bounded out of the window.

"Go," Cole said as he looked behind us to make sure no one else was in the shop.

I hunched down and crawled out of Tattered Pages, dropping a few feet to the frigid ground below me. Poppy immediately hopped into my lap and put her tail right into my face.

"Okay, cat. I get it. You're happy to see me."

Poppy yowled again, and I held her in front of me to make sure whatever was in that canister hadn't affected her. I couldn't see anything wrong with her eyes and she seemed okay.

"That was close, Poppy." I hugged her to me before setting her down beside me.

She butted her head against my waist in apparent agreement.

The sound of sirens echoed through the quiet evening. Cole thumped down on the ground beside me, his eyes watering. He'd stayed in for a hair longer than I had, and the gas must have finally reached him.

I looked out at the back of the strip mall and stilled as I saw a figure running away. I growled under my breath and lurched to my feet. "Stop!" I yelled. I took off after the figure. Logic told me there was no way I'd catch up to the person, but I wanted to do my best. Whoever it was could have killed my cat and me. And Cole. Depending on what was in that canister.

My feet pounded against the concrete and my breath poured out in frigid puffs of air. "Stop!" I called again.

The person running looked back, and I caught a flash of long hair pooling out of the hoodie they wore. It was a woman! Her speed slowed as she turned back around. I pumped my arms and legs, ruing the day I stopped going to the gym, but I was gaining on her.

Someone called my name from behind, but I didn't stop. I wanted this to be over. Right now.

The woman cut through the grass. I gasped as I watched her arms pinwheel around her as she started to slip in the grass. I ran even faster and caught up to her just as she went down, her arms and legs all akimbo.

The hood slid off.

"Carrie!" I shouted.

She squirmed around and tried to get up to run again, but I tackled her as soon as she got one leg up.

Carrie grunted and tried to elbow me in the stomach, but I dodged just in the nick of time. I grunted with pain. No matter where an elbow landed it hurt.

When she finally realized I wasn't letting go, she started to sob hysterically. "I didn't kill her! It was an accident."

Sirens screamed around the corner. I held on tight to Carrie and let out a sigh of relief when I saw a familiar Toyota Avalon come to an abrupt stop a few feet away. Detective Cavanaugh's door flew open, and he rushed over to us, gun drawn.

"Get up, Dakota," he said, his voice menacing.

I turned wide eyes up to him. Fear froze me to the spot. I'd never had a gun pointed at me before and I hoped it would never happen again. Cavanaugh jerked his head to the side, motioning for me to get off of her. I slowly let go and crab walked several feet away before I felt comfortable enough to get up.

"It was Harvey!" she screamed. "Harvey bought the flooring."

My brow wrinkled. What did flooring have to do with it? I glanced around only to see Cole a few feet away giving me a curious look. He raised his hand in a halfhearted wave. I returned it, then squatted down and put my head in my hands.

It took about ten minutes before Hardy came over. By then I was sitting on the cold concrete. He slung his jacket, still warm from his body heat, over my shoulders and sat down beside me.

"I'd like to lecture you about how stupid it was to go after her, but I won't."

A snort escaped me. "Thanks, I guess?"

"Carrie didn't murder her sister," he said. A long sigh escaped him.

"Then who did?"

He spread his feet out in front of him. The sirens on the police cruisers were off now, but the red and blue lights lit up the entire downtown area. Police milled all over the place. Cole was sitting in the back of an ambulance, a green blanket slung across his shoulders. His brows knitted together, and his mouth was a thin slash against his face.

He was saying something, his hands making abrupt motions. An unbidden smile rose on my lips. Cole didn't want to be there anymore than I did. At least he'd have a good story after this. What would I have? A trashed bookstore most likely.

"She set off something in my store. Some kind of gas canister." I rubbed my eyes to wipe away the tears starting to form. "When will I be able to go back into the store?"

He shrugged. "Maybe tomorrow or the next day. Carrie admitted to lacing the books with additional formaldehyde. She figured she could get away with it since printing ink has it in small doses anyway." Hardy tilted his head back to look up at the night sky. His throat worked as he swallowed. "When Marcy got sicker, Carrie was able to get her to sign the power of attorney. But then she got involved with the owner of the investor company."

"She said it was an accident." I pulled Hardy's jacket closer and shuddered in the cold, night air.

"He found out what she had done. When Marcy wanted to put in new laminate flooring, he was able to slide in and underbid the company she initially wanted to use."

Sick realization fluttered in me. "The laminate had additional formaldehyde. I knew it had to be more than the books. Carrie has a degree in chemistry."

Hardy's head jerked down. He stared at me in disbelief. "What a horrible way to go."

"She probably slipped into a coma," I said. I'd briefly studied the effects of formaldehyde in books when I was being certified as an expert in rare books. It happened so little it was just a brief blip in our course. But I remembered now the effects formaldehyde poisoning could have.

"He bought the cheapest laminate he could and had it tested to make sure the levels were harmful before he brought it into the house." Hardy shook his head, a sneer of disgust on his face.

"Carrie wasn't moving fast enough with the deal and if Marcy died, she'd never be able to contest it if she got better."

I hugged myself around the middle, disturbed more than I could communicate with words. Poor Marcy. She never had any control over it and would have never realized what was happening to her. I bet Carrie laced the cheapest books she could while saving all the really valuable ones for herself. But I couldn't be without empathy for Carrie either. She'd been trapped by a man who only wanted money and who blackmailed her to get it.

The entire thing was sickening. "When can I leave?" I asked Hardy.

"Have the EMT's give you an all clear and I'll drop by your house tomorrow for a statement, if that's okay." Hardy's look was one of empathy. "You can file a civil suit for your shop if anything is damaged." He pressed his lips together. "It's going to take a while, but you could get a judgment."

I sighed as he stood up and offered me a hand. I took it, marveling at the warmth of it in this weather. "I have insurance," I said. "I'll think about it."

He clapped a hand on my shoulder. "Good job, Dakota. I hope next time we don't have to meet like this." Hardy left me standing there still clutching his jacket around my shoulders. I wasn't sure what that meant, but it sounded like he wanted to meet me again, away from all of this. A smile peeked out from my mouth as I straightened and made my way over to Cole.

When he saw me, his face brightened, and he held out his blanket as an offering to share his warmth. I hopped up on the back of the ambulance and let him wrap an arm around me.

"Thanks for getting us out of there." I hadn't seen

Poppy since I'd chased after Carrie, but I knew she was around here somewhere, probably getting into mischief.

Cole ducked his head awkwardly. Even through the flashing lights, I could see his face color. It was surprisingly cute.

"It was nothing." Cole's shoulders dropped. "This is kind of crazy, right?"

I looked out at the overwhelming police force and shrugged. "Murders rarely happen in Silverwood Hollow, right?"

Cole's gaze was thoughtful. "Let's hope not," he said.

I shivered at the ominous tone of his words. Let's hope not, indeed.

EPILOGUE

Corky was tipsy already, her wrinkled face flushed with color and a wide, happy grin on her face. Trudy sat beside her, her hair done up in a messy bun and her hands wrapped around a large mug with steam curling from the top.

I sat beside them, enjoying a sip of mulled wine, a recipe made by a local. It was fruit and spicy and probably spiked with a hair too much brandy.

Harper stood by Jeff a few feet away, their heads together discussing something intently. I still wasn't sure how I felt about those two, but it wasn't my business. Harper was a grown woman and Jeff seemed less annoying with her in his life, so I'd wait and watch.

The main street of Silverwood Hollow was shut down to traffic. Every shop, even the old knife seller's, was decorated to the hilt with fall colors. Brown and orange fairy lights bathed the town in a soft dewy glow and the gray clouds had lifted for a glorious few hours.

Mom and Gran were somewhere around here. Gran mentioned moving back here and I was half delighted, half terrified. She'd cornered Hardy when she got here this morning and gleefully berated him for several minutes about why he didn't want to date her granddaughter. I grinned at him and waggled my fingers before I'd left him to her mercy.

Every time I thought about the look of homicide in his eyes as they begged me not to leave him, I laughed. Gran traipsed by after that laughing as he stood by watching her back wearing a bemused expression. That was Gran for you.

Cole was somewhere around, too. He'd been subdued when I congratulated him on the front-page story that came out the day after I'd tackled Carrie. You would have thought with how hard he hounded me to get information, he'd be ecstatic, but something about it was bothering him.

They'd arrested Harvey Crouch for first-degree murder, though none of us were sure the charges would stick considering how he'd done it. If they could prove he knew the laminate was contaminated along with the books, they might have a chance. I'd run into Hardy a few days afterward and his viewpoint was grim. He was confident he'd find something to stick, but he didn't know how long of a sentence it would net.

Carrie was released on bond and required to stay in her house. I hadn't seen her since and I didn't want to. The entire thing was still keeping me up at night. She was still the sole heir of their fortune and it was maddening to see her, in essence, being rewarded for it.

When I expressed my concerns to Hardy, he'd smiled, though it didn't look happy. He assured me a large chunk of it would be going to legal fees. It was a small comfort.

I took another sip of the boozy mulled wine and smiled as I looked out at the bustling town. The air was even colder now, forcing me to don my wool hat, best coat, and most insulated gloves. It wasn't snowing yet, but the bite in the air told me it wasn't far away.

The sound of a voice clearing startled me. I looked to my right and Cole stood there. He held a mug of something steaming and was pulling a chair to sit down beside me.

"You're going to be volunteered as a pie taster if you sit here for too long," I quipped. "One of the judges woke up with a stomach virus and couldn't make it."

An endearing grin split his face at the thought. "Sign me up! As long as there's apple pie."

I scoffed. "Of course, there is."

He sat close enough for our arms to brush together. I didn't know what I thought about Cole after everything that happened. He'd protected me in a heated moment, even if he'd been a thorn in my side before that.

Maybe we could be friends.

Cole noticed my scrutiny and clinked his mug against mine gently. "Friends?" he asked hopefully.

I nodded. "Friends." I looked away; the comforting presence of the journalist-made-friend beside me.

A warm, cozy feeling grew in my body as I watched my friends and family having a wonderful time. Laughter and conversation bubbled around me and a sense of contentment filled me.

This was my home. I had a place here and I couldn't wait to see what the future held.

———

THE SECOND SHELF Indulgence mystery is now available! For more Dakota and Poppy, click HERE!

ALSO BY S.E. BABIN

A Shelf Indulgence Cozy Mystery Series

How about a ghost whisperer in a new magical town? Check out
The Psychic Cleaner series!

Psychic Cleaner

Like a little more magic with your cozies? Check out The
Magical Soapmaker Mysteries!

The Magical Soapmaker Mysteries

If you'd like a little more action and sass and don't mind some
PG-13 language, check out my Aphrodite series.

The Goddess Chronicles

Or, if you like a snarky bartender with a secretive mixed heritage,
meet Violet!

Cocktails in Hell

ABOUT THE AUTHOR

Sheryl is a spy and currently on the run. She supports herself through her mystery writing endeavors.

Follow her on Amazon at: https://www.amazon.com/S-E-Babin/e/B00J1J236A